George Nicholson

Fifty Years in South Africa

Being Some Recollections and Reflections of a Veteran Pioneer

George Nicholson

Fifty Years in South Africa
Being Some Recollections and Reflections of a Veteran Pioneer

ISBN/EAN: 9783337004675

Printed in Europe, USA, Canada, Australia, Japan

Cover: Foto ©Raphael Reischuk / pixelio.de

More available books at **www.hansebooks.com**

FIFTY YEARS IN SOUTH AFRICA:

Being some Recollections and Reflections of a
Veteran Pioneer.

BY

G. NICHOLSON.

ILLUSTRATED.

LONDON:

W. W. GREENER.

1898.

FIFTY YEARS IN SOUTH AFRICA.

CONTENTS.

CHAPTER I.

INTRODUCTORY.

CHAPTER II.

FIRST YEARS IN SOUTH AFRICA.

CHAPTER III.

GAME AND SPORT IN SOUTH AFRICA.

CHAPTER IV.

LIONS.

CHAPTER IX.

HOW THE DIAMOND FIELDS WERE ACQUIRED BY ENGLAND.

CHAPTER X.

THE TRANSVAAL.

CHAPTER XI.

RHODESIA.

Fifty Years in South Africa.

INTRODUCTION.

MANY books have been written about South Africa. Its people, its resources, its politics, and more particularly its future as part of the British Empire, are of ever increasing interest, and no apology is needed for any writer who has had long acquaintance and intimate knowledge of the Colonies stating his experiences and opinions. The author is a man who has lived the ordinary life of a South African pioneer settler; for more than half a century his interests have been identical with those of the Colonists, and he, if anyone, is able to judge from actual experience, what may be beneficial and what has proved harmful. Unlike many who have written on South African affairs, he has " no axe to grind," has no prejudices, and whatever there may be of bias in his arguments pro and con the claims of Uitlander and Boer is but the natural outcome of a long study of evidence received at first hand in daily intercourse with men belonging to different races and parties. As an expert, his opinion deserves attention and his suggestions for ameliorating the present tension merit consideration.

No one can read the chapters on game and shooting without being convinced that although a hunter for the market the author is a thorough sportsman. Of personal adventures he is slow to write, remarking that one episode is very much the same as another; many sportsmen will regret that one who has killed so many lions and much other large game is so reticent on the subject of his sporting exploits, but those who intend visiting South Africa in search of sport will read with greater profit the particulars he gives of the game-lands, and his remarks on the subject of game preservation should be borne in mind by those who have the interest of South Africa at heart. To the Boer large game has been a source of wealth, and its rapid extinction in the Transvaal will probably result at no distant date in a " trek " of the Boer stock-raisers to districts within British territory, and this must react on the division of parties within the Transvaal and so has a political as well as an economical aspect.

It is the intending emigrant the author more particularly addresses. His advice to those about to try their fortune in South Africa is pertinent and sound. In no sense can he be considered an emigration agent; he has the interests of his adopted country at heart, and wishes to attract those only who are likely to succeed and make the Colonies more prosperous, and at the same time better their own positions. In his desire to disillusion the sanguine he may have coloured too darkly the difficulties which beset the intrepid settler, but, in all, there is nothing set forth that will deter those of the right sort who resolve to make a fair livelihood in South Africa, and there is much that will help them to decide upon the best districts, seasons, and means for making a beginning.

The author's simple recountal of his journeyings and doings in the Great Thirst Land and on the banks of the Limpopo bring vividly to mind the wild, weird, waterless waste of sand dunes and the thick jungles on its eastern edge. His recollections of the immense herds of large game on the veldt and the mention of his intercourse with hunters like Gordon Cumming and Oswell are as interesting as instructive. We seem to see these mighty hunters, and the shadowy form of the intrepid explorer, David Livingstone, standing before the erect and wiry man who writes of him. The native Kaffirs, the bastard Hottentots and wild bushmen gather round his lumbering ox-drawn waggon as it is slowly moving across the loose stones and sand of the grassless burning waste. Thrilling in its simplicity is the description of the flight by moonlight from the Transvaal in the time of war, and no mere multiplication of words could give the imaginative reader a better idea of the crude, ignorant, retiring Boer than the outline the author has given when seen by the sidelights he has thrown upon his family life, his religion, and his hopes of betterment. In reading what the author has written one feels that it is not of the Boer he is learning, but that it is the Boer himself with whom he is brought face to face. And what is true in respect of the Dutch race in like manner applies to the rest of the book; it is in truth Africa in its crude reality—that, and no more.

THE EDITOR.

PREFACE.

THIS little book owes its existence to what is usually called an accident. It came about in this way. A gentleman, personally unknown to me, himself an author, very kindly sent me a copy of one of his works on a technical subject of interest to me, and the fact of this book having reached its sixth edition is a sufficient proof of its merits. As some little return for this act of kindness, I posted to him a bundle of the MS. memoranda into which this book has developed. I acceded to my friend's request to publish, and agreed to furnish him with some additional copy, so as to bring it up to date.

If the public endorse my editor's opinion of this crude attempt to amuse or interest some of them, one more pleasure will have been added to those enjoyed by one who is now far on his way to complete an existence passed among three generations of fellow mortals of divers colours and nationalities.

The natural "camaraderie" of my brother sportsmen induces me to hope that they at least will treat my shortcomings leniently.

Of the sympathies of Exeter Hall enthusiasts I hardly hope to be a recipient: for they are generally as cocksure of the infallibility of their own fads as if their community consisted wholly of Popes, and I have my doubts as to the validity of their claims. Anyhow, I hear that my editor has excised many of my remarks on missionary enterprise in South Africa. I endorse his action, without, however, altering my private opinions—which do not count.

I am no enemy to Missions quâ Missions, and these remarks mostly applied to a past period, when the chief occupation of the reverend functionaries seemed directed towards accentuating the normal antipathies between the white and coloured races. Undoubtedly too many missionaries of former days used their alleged converts as tools to obstruct trade, a good deal of which they for a time monopolised by these means. At present such practices are no longer in vogue, and the personnel of the missionary enterprise are most respectable men. However, the consensus of South African opinion seems to be that but little beneficial impression has been made on the pure African negro race, whatever may be said on the subject in regard to benefits conferred on and accepted by the " off-coloured " Colonial population.

As regards my dissertations on outstanding disputes between the Imperial Government and the Transvaal Autocrat, I can only hope they may give effect to criticism, and thus draw public opinion.

The notes on the prospects of the Chartered Company's Territory (Rhodesia) may be read with advantage by intending investors and settlers; and my opinion of the country is, shortly, that its prosperity as a field for European immigrants is dependent on the amount of its possible gold output, but that from an African point of view, it being a fairly well watered land, superior as regards its capabilities for stock-raising and agriculture to most other parts of South Africa, it will at no distant date attract a considerable population of Africanders, both of Boer and English blood.

Finally, I trust that the reader will perceive that I have not written up to any special objective, but with a view to express honest opinions, in it may be rather blunt terms. And here, perhaps, it will be as well to mention that I have no pecuniary interests in South Africa, but, notwithstanding this deficiency, the welfare of the country enlists my sincerest best wishes.

G. NICHOLSON.

ROBERTSON, CAPE COLONY.

FIFTY YEARS IN SOUTH AFRICA.

CHAPTER I.

EARLY RECOLLECTIONS.

OVER sixty years have passed since I was a Cantab of Trinity Hall, and during this time greater changes in political and social life have been wrought than in any other like term at any previous period.

I did not care for the life of a London resident. I had a fixed aversion to crowds indoors; avoided balls, theatres, and frivolities generally. Studying law was not more to my fancy, and my chief amusement was fencing, which I took up with great zest, frequenting Angelo's Rooms, near the Horse Guards. There I met few men who could successfully compete with me, and but one who could beat me easily. This was Sir George Duckett, a short, middle-aged man of great strength

B

and remarkable activity—in fact, the best man with the foils I ever met.

Of soldiers and sailors, of English country life, too, I saw a good deal. At my father's place in Devonshire, and elsewhere, I met such well-known people as Sir Robert Peel, Bulwer, Lord Mahon, Lord Melbourne, and the great and good "Iron Duke," and many of his Peninsula and Waterloo heroes.

Often I would take a trip to Greenwich, for a long chat with some of the armless or legless old pensioners who had fought under Nelson and other naval heroes of the great war. Of these veterans there were at that time two thousand comfortably cared for in the grand old palace, and it was delightful to sit under a tree in the park and, while filling their pipes with the best tobacco, listen to the well-told yarns of these cheery old Vikings, whose conversation was far more instructive than that with which one is usually bored in more polished circles. With many of the non-commissioned military officers of the armies led by Wellington in the Peninsula and at Waterloo I struck up a close acquaintance and acquired much information. These men generally were remarkable for broader views than their fellow heroes in the naval service, and I especially remember three of them—Sergeant-Major Fairbrother, of the Life Guards; Sergeant Biggs, 14th Light Dragoons; and Sergeant-Major Robertshaw, Life Guards—all fine men physically, in the prime of life, and of superior intelligence. Fairbrother and Biggs died in the service of two of our titled landed proprietors, as land stewards with salaries of £500 a year. Robertshaw was a fine old soldier, but a "roué," and was comfortably settled as instructor of a yeomanry regiment, and died in that service. Biggs was attacked at Waterloo when temporarily separated from his regiment by three Cuirassiers, all of whom he killed. His Colonel had his sabre engraved with an account of the exploit on the blade, which I have often handled. I remember being much impressed with one of his remarks to the effect that if we had had a cavalry force equal in numbers to that of the enemy at Waterloo, we should have won the battle in two hours, because our cavalry would at least have neutralised that of the enemy, and enabled our infantry to fight continuously in line, and thus inflict fearful loss on the French who attacked in columns. As it was the French cavalry were able to force our infantry into squares, when, of course, their offensive powers were minimised and their losses increased by artillery fire.

I was a good horseman, a crack shot, and unusually strong and active for a man who never weighed more than 164 lb. in his best days. Coarse dissipation was never a. temptation to me, and all kinds of gambling distasteful, nor were society's frivolities much more attractive.

Law I hated from my soul, and although I had exceptional opportunities of a brilliant career by following its thorny and miry ways, I threw away the unwelcome chances, and hankered after a life of adventure and more freedom than is consistent with existence in civilised lands.

In 1830 I went to Paris on a visit to Bishop Luscombe, in company with my father and a Mr. Kemble; during our stay there the Revolution by which Charles lost his crown occurred.

On the first of the three days' battle we were returning from a visit to a château some miles from the city, and when near the Champs Elysées were startled on hearing heavy firing in the direction of the Place Vendôme, near which was our hotel.

There was nothing for it but to endeavour to reach it and get shelter as soon as possible. Our hired carriage was seized by the insurgents, and we were politely but firmly ordered away—the carriage being wanted to add to a barricade. There was a good deal of firing going on between the troops and the mob all round. I remember noticing the blue marks made by the bullets which struck the pavement, and the appearance of wounded men slowly trickling out of the fight. Being foreigners, we were not molested, but rather assisted on our way by the mob, and at last reached the corner of the Rue de la Paix, but found it impossible to get to our quarters in the Place Vendôme, where a furious battle between the Royal Guards and the mob was just beginning.

In spite of the surrounding terrors, any number of heedless gamins were mixed up with the combatants, and seemed to enjoy the hubbub immensely—although every now and then one of them would fall from a shot, and die murmuring a farewell to his mother, who is much more sacred to the average Frenchman than " le bon Dieu " himself. Our party came in for lots of chaff from these gamins, and Kemble, who, like Saul, towered a full head and shoulders above everybody—standing about 6 ft. 7 in.—and a very fine man to boot, came in for more than his share, but retaliated with effect, and was rapidly becoming inconveniently popular when we were obliged to halt now and then under shelter to let a passing shower of mitraille and bullets pass by. By dodging into doorways and taking such chances to progress as we could, we at length found temporary lodgings in a small hotel where Kemble was known. It was not far from the Tuileries, and it served us until the long battle ended and the crown of the Bourbons passed to the newer régime.

On subsequent visits to Paris I was very much struck with the superior taste in costume shown by the French working classes, in contrast with English of the same grade. The French workman aims at appearing what he is, and on Sunday and other gala days in a neat cap and a clean blouse is a far more agreeable spectacular object than the English workman encased in a bad copy of the costume of a higher class, including a cheap and hideous "top-hat," generally a misfit, and evidently very uncomfortable, but none the less an object of worship to its suffering wearer. And then the "grisette"—small, sallow, and seldom pretty—she trips along with infinite grace in the neat and tasteful costume of her class, and is far more attractive than her insular sister, albeit the latter is generally of superior physique and good looks, but spoils all by a vulgar unsuccessful attempt at copying the costume of the classes above her, and only succeeds in exhibiting herself as the personification of a fraud, often slatternly, and always pretentious and vulgar. Chat for five minutes with a French "grisette," and you will find that she can speak her own language pleasantly and correctly. Converse with an English girl of the same class, and you will hear Cockneyisms which will make you wish you were deaf.

At this period Paris, taken as a whole, was by no means a handsome city; its best and brightest quarters were but of relatively small extent. Grouped, however, as these parts were, closely together, and visible almost at a glance by visitors, the effect of the first sight of the place was certainly cheery, and at the same time imposing; and as the visitor's carriage rolled down the Champs Elysées, along the Rue de Rivoli, and through the

Place Vendôme on to the boulevards, he could not but feel that he was gazing on a charming picture. The rest of the vast city consisted mainly of very narrow streets, bordered by high houses, and were without any foot-pavement for the comfort and protection of the pedestrian. Down the middle of each street was a malodorous sewer, and at distant intervals dingy-looking oil-lamps swung on cords, and by night served only to make darkness visible.

Coming from England, one missed the numerous neat and well-finished carriages, splendidly horsed, common then with us. In Paris, rope traces generally formed part of the harness of the few carriages to be seen, and the horses were either round, chubby Norman cobs—good enough in their way, but decidedly out of place in anything but a country cart—or were lean, gaunt equine specimens of a washy nondescript breed, un-attractive and dejected in aspect. To compensate for these things, every one seemed light-hearted and cheerful, with little to do—and doing that little rather as if acting in a drama than as a serious matter of business. " Vive la bagatelle! " seemed to be the universal motto; young as I was, I was much interested by witnessing its practical application on a national scale. Here and there only was a horseman to be seen, and he almost invariably turned out to be an Englishman who had brought his own cattle and eccentricities across the Channel wherewith to astonish the natives.

A happy interlude of travel and sport in the Scottish Highlands occurred in 1837, and this started again my natural bent for adventure.

I never cared for the usual school games, such as cricket, football, or, indeed, any pastime involving disciplined action. Boating I delighted in, and could manage a small craft under sail or oar to perfection. At the University I occasionally pulled an oar in our college boat, and participated in several winning races (bumps), but much preferred solitary excursions. Of archery I was passionately fond—not in the shape of formal target-shooting, but when roaming away over the fields, practising at any tempting mark, and doing a little poaching when opportunity offered. A pheasant or two, or a hare, killed with my bow afforded more pleasure than a whole bagful obtained with the gun. Sometimes a little mischief tempted me while out with the bow, and once I tried a long pull at a huge pig, which fell to the shot. However, I sought the irate owner and got out of the scrape by paying rather more than the value of the animal.

Experience proved to me that many of the marvellous feats attributed to ancient archers, disbelieved in by modern votaries of the art, are nevertheless approximately true, making, of course, a little occasional allowance for an abnormal pull at the "long bow" by the historians. If any modern archer should read this, he will know that a bow with a pull of between fifty and sixty pounds is quite as strong as an average man can effectually use, but it must be allowed that practice is now only occasional, and merely intended to facilitate "hits" at the target, whereas not only accuracy but range were desiderata when the bow was a weapon of war, and the art of shooting was practised with a view to the attainment of success on those lines. By practice I eventually found that a bow of ninety-five pounds draw was quite within manageable limits; that a range of four hundred yards could be attained; and that at forty or fifty yards an arrow with a square pyramidal steel head could be sent through an iron spade.

For foxhunting I never cared much, as the ostentation, the crowd, and the absence of opportunity for the exercise of any individual hunting instincts in the participator were distasteful concomitants. To be obliged to concentrate all one's energies and strain the powers of one's horse in overcoming artificial obstructions, to the exclusion of any of the more legitimate operations of real hunting, seemed to verge on boredom, and hardly repaid one for wearing the conspicuous red coat and uncomfortable leg-gear.

CHAPTER II.

FIRST YEARS IN SOUTH AFRICA.

IN January, 1844, I found myself on board ship, beating out against a tremendous adverse gale across the Bay of Biscay, bound for the Cape—which we reached early in March.

Cape Town in those days was a quiet, prosperous, but old-fashioned non-progressive place. The coloured working population, principally of Malay extraction, wore a costume of their own, and looked wonderfully clean and well fed. There seemed to be an entire absence of bustle or hurry, and soon after the noontide meal every one turned in for a comfortable " siesta," which possibly accounted in some measure for the total absence of that haggard, worn expression so observable in most of the urban inhabitants of all classes at home. A few substantial merchant firms, headed by courteous well-bred gentlemen, transacted the extensive wholesale and shipping business of the place, and, strange to say, the ordinary official classes repudiated the manners and customs of bumbledom, and were genial and polite. Showy plate-glassed shop fronts were unknown, but a sufficiency of dark, cool retail shops, containing good stocks, supplied luxuries and necessaries at moderate prices. Upon the whole, the place, with its surrounding villages, villas, and climate, impressed the visitor pleasantly, notwithstanding a great dearth of hotels, the paucity of the clerical element, and the prevalence of that quiet content which the modern age of progress abhors.

At that time—and until the overland route to India was available—the Cape was the great sanitarium where military and civil officers of the Honourable East India Company came to recover from wounds or to freshen up exhausted constitutions. Some two thousand of these visitors, with wives and families in proportion, enlivened the place, and circulated a very appreciable amount of welcome coin while recovering their health. Tasteful carriages, well horsed, and driven by stately Indian coachmen clad in turbans and spotless white muslin, were numerous in the town and suburbs; railways were unknown, and active little Cape hacks were the general locomotive factors employed by the more sturdy classes. Society was based on unostentatious principles; manners were decidedly better than those of the modern type, and morals probably no worse, although less encased in the fortifications of more modern cant and pretension. A member of the heroic Napier family, who had left an arm on one of the grand battlefields of the Peninsula, worthily represented Royalty, and made the shabby old Government House a pleasant and hospitable centre liberally accessible.

On the Cape flats jackals did duty for foxes, and were hunted by a good subscription pack, well ridden to by a not too numerous field, including both sexes. Some of the good old Cape Dutch families—now, I regret to say, hustled out of the position they then so worthily occupied—allowed their charming daughters, splendidly mounted, to participate in the pleasures of hunting and flirtation. One of these young Africanders captured an English military officer—the heir to a dukedom—and would no doubt have fulfilled perfectly all the wifely and aristocratic duties of a duchess had not a hard fate and a swift transport ship intervened to forbid the banns.

All these things are mere matters of memory; most, if not all, of the gallant men and charming women are in the "Land of the Leal," but not yet forgotten by the solitary survivor. Meanwhile responsible government has been acquired, and as one of the results a heavy debt weighs the taxpayer down—bankruptcy once impended, and could not have been averted but for the timely discovery of the diamond fields—long lines of railroad have been constructed; fine public buildings and grand hotels erected; magnificent fast steamships ply to and from the Table Bay; capacious docks afford shelter from the terrific north-west hurricanes which are imminent at certain seasons, and were formerly terribly destructive. Tramways and cabs abound in the city and its suburbs; gas and electric lights dispel the darkness of the old-time nights; and aggregate wealth has been largely increased no doubt. As a natural consequence, millionaires have been evolved, and the struggle of life has been painfully intensified for those who do not belong to that species; dire poverty exhibits ghastly evidences of its prevalence, and coarse vice is obtrusively apparent.

Crowds of the unemployed, too often invalids,

who have come out in search of a genial climate and suitable work, loaf about helpless and hungry; unless the sextons of the cemeteries can account for their disappearance at intervals, their fate is likely to remain an unsolved mystery in the majority of cases.

South Africa is not the place for such immigrants, and indeed the existing fixed population is more than numerous and capable enough to supply any present or probable demands for work of any kind. Whether upon the whole this state of things is preferable to that of the olden time, when none were very rich and none painfully poor, I decline to assert. I may, however, avow a personal preference for a life of reasonable content, with easy labour, to one involving any amount of deferred hope expended in a fearful struggle, and terminated too often by heart-sickness and despair.

Well, after a pleasant sojourn in and around the Cape for some months, I got on board the old Phœnix steamer, bound for Algoa Bay. This little ship was a model of comfort and safety, commanded by a genial captain named Harrington, and was the only coasting steamer then on the coast.

A more dreary looking place than Port Elizabeth could hardly be imagined. The town consisted of substantial stone-built barracks for a detachment of troops, the Phœnix Hotel, a general store or two, a post-office, some three or four private residences scattered about among barren sand dunes and pretty close to the furious breakers for which the bay is notorious. Whether there was a church and the orthodox drinking-bar I forget, as I was not addicted to frequenting such places.

This place I left as soon as possible, and went on to the then pretty and primitive village of Uitenhague. Here gardens, fruit, and greenery prevailed; a comfortable inn kept by a worthy English couple provided for one's wants amply, and I stopped for two months, enjoying, at first, some excellent bush-buck and snipe shooting, then afterwards got a fine lion and several buffalo, about twenty miles from the village.

Hyænas used to come to the outskirts of the village in such numbers that one moonlight night I killed seven of them as they arrived in detachments to gorge on a dead horse.

Later I bought three good horses, and started for Graaf-Reinet, which pretty village I reached

in about three days. I had a Hottentot "after-
rider" with me, and was armed with a good double
gun. The spare horse carried blankets, a change
of clothes, and some food; we had, too, a small
sharp axe wherewith to cut thorny bushes to form
a defence for ourselves and the horses from the
very possible attacks of lions or hyænas at night.

During the first day's journey I shot a fine cow
elephant with good tusks, which was standing
knee-deep in a muddy pool close to our track.
Creeping up to within a few yards, I got a side-shot
at the head between the eye and the ear, and the
huge beast collapsed at once. We could not then
spare time to cut out the ivory, but having marked
the tusks—which the Hottentot told me nobody
would then abstract—we left them till our return
journey, and then easily drew them out by hand,
as not a particle of flesh was left on the skeleton
—the vultures, wild beasts, and corruption having
completely denuded the bones.

I shall never forget our first night's bivouac in
the veldt, near a large pool of water in thick bush.
Having made a strong kraal for the protection of
ourselves and horses, and collected plenty of dry
wood for keeping up the fire all night, I felt fairly

easy till darkness came on, when the whole neighbourhood seemed to swarm with animals coming to quench their thirst at the pool. Fiendish hyænas made the air tremble with their loud, weird howls, varied at intervals by indulgence in the peculiar tittering laugh characteristic of their base race; jackals joined in additional discordant vocal performances; and a few lions roared magnificently at intervals. A troop of elephants came to the water, and could be heard splashing about, at times uttering a peculiar squealing noise indicative perhaps of enjoyment. I can't boast of having felt easy enough to make an attempt at sleep, but busied myself in keeping up a blazing fire during the greater part of the night, and occasionally fired a shot when the lions came too near. As for my yellow attendant, he took these things as a matter of course, and although he did not sleep much, was evidently quite indemnified by an indulgence in unlimited coffee and tobacco, with a " soupie " of the beloved " Cape Smoke " which I threw in. I got a couple of hours' sleep after the bright morning star appeared, and, having let our horses graze a bit, as soon as it was light enough to do so safely, we started in the early sunshine, and soon reached a Boer farm, where we got some forage for the nags, and some hot milk and rusks for breakfast.

After this the country became more open, and at distant intervals we found farm shanties, or Boer camps, and although ostriches and spring-bucks were plentiful on all sides, we heard no more lions; soon I learned to despise the cowardly hyænas which howled round our sleeping quarters, for I preferred the ground to those offered by the kindly but not very cleanly Boers.

Having passed a few days in Graaff Reinet, I crossed the great Sneeberg range to look at a farm, which I shortly bought for £2,000, and stocked with 4,000 sheep, 150 head of horned cattle, and sixty horses of sorts. The farm consisted of about 30,000 acres of mountain and plain, with about two and a half acres of arable land near the house—this, rough but comfortable enough. There was water sufficient for the stock, but none available for the indispensable irrigation of more arable land than the patch mentioned.

Here I vegetated for two years; then sold the place and stock at a good profit, and shortly cleared out for the interior.

On and around this farm black gnus and spring-buck grazed in thousands on the plains; among the mountains rhebuck and klipspringer were to be had; leopards and hyænas added to its sporting charms; and bustards of various species, francolin, and quail abounded. Whilst there I longed to explore the then mysterious interior, and in due time, well equipped with waggons, draught oxen, horses, and all necessaries, crossed the Orange River, beyond which, to unknown distances, native rule—or misrule—prevailed in all directions. Little Boer Republics in an embryonic and tentative condition, in the territories now known as the Orange Free State and Transvaal, were in course of incubation; here and there small parties of leather-breeched, semi-nomadic whites were to be met with, and, if possible, " passed by " by any one at all sensitive in the matter of dirt and rags. Missionary stations, too, were pushing onwards, and, to my great surprise, the Gospellic adven-turers in charge, instead of being, as I had been led to suppose from glancing at some of their literature, overworked and underfed crossbearers, were enjoying a good deal more of leisure and comfort than people of their class could have attained to at home.

I do not pretend to appraise the value of the spiritual results of African missions, but my impression is that if their cost was judiciously applied to ameliorate the social and moral conditions of our myriads of home-bred heathen, the money would be better employed, and yield a more abundant harvest in far more important localities.

In 1845-46 the plains of the Orange Free State were covered with herds of gnus, Burchell's zebras, blesbuck, and springbuck in numbers which, if approximately hinted at now with absolute truth, would wrinkle the countenance of the reader with a derisive smile. These plains were very well supplied with water, either in the form of rivulets or chains of deep pools, and the herbage, though kept short by the game herds, looked infinitely superior to any I had seen within Colonial limits. Here and there quaint rock mounds and low stony ridges dotted over more or less with bush varied the scene, and afforded well-tenanted lairs to the numerous lions and other predatories, whose abundant food supplies were always within easy grip. It was indeed a charming loafing-ground for any man of contemplative instincts dashed with hunting proclivities. I spent many enjoyable months on these plains, shooting just enough game to supply camp requirements, and now and then going in for a lion-hunt by way of a little desirable excitement. On that trip twenty-seven of these animals fell to my double smooth-bore flint-and-steel "Purdey" in seven days' shooting, besides a few others at odd times. So numerous, indeed, were they, that once, near Kaffir River, I counted over forty of all sizes in a single troop. Wart hogs, too, abounded and afforded good bursts for a mile or so, when they generally came to bay and fell to the thrusts of a bayonet fixed on a bamboo shaft —a poor substitute for a spear, but the best at hand.

A large section of what is now the Orange Free State then belonged to a Hottentot tribe under Adam Kok, whose capital was a village called Phillipolis. These people professed Christianity, and upon the whole were not a bad lot. Some of them were rich in flocks and herds, and one I knew possessed about five hundred horses, mostly of a useful, hardy stamp, many of which were admirably broken in as shooting horses, cheap at £10 usually asked for them. No visible poverty of depravity was observable, as "Cape Smoke" was, if not an unknown, at least a very scarce article of consumption.

Since those days Adam Kok's territory has been sold to the Orange Free State, and he and his people removed to the coast between Natal and the Kaffir tribes on the eastern frontiers of Cape Colony. This yellow race displays essentially imitative tendencies when brought into contact with white people, and as a consequence has decreased in numbers by at least 90 per cent. within the last fifty years ; indeed, within Colonial limits a pure-bred Hottentot is now very rarely seen. As servants in many capacities they were far superior to Kaffirs, excelling more especially as grooms, trackers of lost cattle, shikar work, and so forth.

They might easily have been saved from extinction by appropriate legislation, but the anti-slavery enthusiasts insisted on drastic treatment, and the poor " Tottie " succumbed to a full dose of freedom, administered without timely preparation. Whether the darker-coloured aboriginal African races will ever adopt our form of civilisation or not is problematical. Shoddy specimens of converted Kaffirs in considerable numbers are on show at missionary centres, and while kept "kraalled" within institutional limits they look very like the real article, but once outside the sacred limits the veneer is found to be very thin, and the missionary product compares unfavourably with his more simple heathen brethren in their normal state. Exceptions there are no doubt, but exceptional excellence on the lines I am treating of is but rarely worth its cost price, and does not much influence the general quality of the output.

The reading of the social barometer (1894) indicates approximate perils, the advent of which will probably lower values all round in England, and gradually convert the possession of riches into that of competence, and poverty will mean a graduated scale of pauperism, arising in some measure from what we call natural causes, but accentuated to an acute degree by the short-sighted and hysterical legislation of these modern days. Far from being in a position to throw away money to pay for the assumed spiritual necessities of African races, every available fraction of it will be less than enough to provide for the bodily necessities of an excessive population mainly owing its origin to an artificially stimulated system of manufactures and commerce, successful for a longer period than might have been expected, but now on the down grade of gradual decay owing to successful and ever-increasing foreign competition, which is itself based on the cheaper wages at which foreign labour is obtainable.

Radical changes in the political programme touching foreign affairs, although severely ignored by public opinion, are answerable for the deadlock in commerce now soon to become a sad fact— unless trade reports are mere printed sheets published by the father of lies himself or by a very apt staff of his subordinate employees. For a long period, to be counted by generations, England steadily pursued a course of foreign policy having for its aim the perpetuation of a state of unrest and war on the Continent, which she successfully carried out, not without great cost, but still within limits which permitted a very sensible increase in wealth, population, and prestige.

Geographical position counted for much of the success attained by acting on the lines of policy indicated, and people troubled themselves very little about the morality or otherwise involved.

In, or rather shortly after, 1815 England had

obtained about all she wanted, and was desirous of gathering up and employing her loot to the best advantage, and soon bloomed into the position of the autocrat of the world's commerce. The élite of the Continental populations had been sacrificed on the war altar, and of capital for industrial purposes little was available. In view of recently passed experiences and of minatory prospects, the necessary capital for manufacturing and commercial enterprise was unobtainable abroad; England plied her work unmolested by competition, and many years elapsed before foreign capital accumulated and driblets of it were applied to the exigencies of trade developments. America, too, was only in its adolescence, and but yesterday, counted by historical periods, attained the giant station and strength which now characterise her as a nation, bringing qualities which bid fair shortly to enable her successfully to defy competition in all fields of production.

The moral of this digression is that in view of the natural and apparent course of events it would seem prudent for John Bull to diminish, or, better still, forego, expensive luxuries in the unproductive regions of Negrophilism, not forgetting meanwhile to practise all other possible economies in other directions.

And now I am sure the time has fully come to offer my best apologies to the reader for very numerous and disorderly digressions, past, present, and to come, which I trust will be accepted on the plea that I have no claim to belong even to the rank and file of the disciplined corps of littérateurs, and that they flow from my pen without premeditation, and guiltless of malice prepense.

The period between this first trip and 1848 was spent in a succession of journeys both in and outside the Cape Colony, during which, as an amateur, I saw a little of the operations of the great Kaffir war in the East Province, and in self-defence had to kill two of the native warriors, who, if they had not been vile shots, ought to have settled my affairs in this world. My custom there was, when in thick bush, to carry a double 12-bore gun, one barrel loaded with ball and the other with a charge of S.S.G. shot, and the latter charge proved most effective up to about sixty yards.

I had visited the Limpopo, killed a number of elephants, rhinos, buffaloes, and other big game which then swarmed on its banks, and made the acquaintance of Gordon Cummings, Dr. Livingstone, and Mr. Oswell.

Cummings did not strike me as a man with whom any one would care to become intimate. He was a mighty hunter, and although the book he wrote was supposed by critics to contain a good many "unveracities," I don't think such was the case; none of his performances in the hunting-field amounted to much more than usually fell to the lot of most sporting wanderers in the same localities. As an elephant hunter he was certainly not A1, as any one may gather from his own accounts of the number of shots he usually fired before bringing his quarry to the ground. In fact, when in pursuit of very large game he was handicapped by his weight in the saddle and by his habit of using a rifle, that weapon in those days being a very inferior arm to a smooth bore, as it could not be used with a sufficient charge of powder to ensure the necessary amount of penetration.

Oswell, on the contrary, was a very light weight, a splendid horseman, always well mounted, and invariably shot with a smooth 10-bore, which in his hands made short work of all kinds of big game. Indeed Oswell, as an all-round man, was hard to equal and more difficult to beat—a grand specimen of a thorough cultured English gentleman. Brave he was to the verge of temerity, but brimming over with kind-heartedness, courtesy, and geniality. He died only three or four years ago, much regretted by every one who knew him, but hardly known to any outside his own small circle.

The world owes more to him than it is aware of, as he was the first man to appreciate the great qualities of Livingstone, who was indebted to him for the necessary outfit with which to commence his wonderful career as an explorer.

Livingstone was a little, dark, tough-looking man, with a countenance every lineament of which denoted the possession of courage, pertinacity, and intellect. He, in common with his kind, had his faults too, and had he not been a sincere Christian, my impression is that a competitor in his own peculiar vocation would have met with but little mercy if he crossed his path. Personally, the little intercourse I had with Livingstone was very pleasant, but then I do not belong to the competitive order, and am anything but ambitious of notoriety even of the best quality, and therefore do not clash with those who are.

Now any old—or, for that matter, young—lady may travel over the length and breadth of South Africa with as much safety from human annoyance as in any part of the world perhaps, quite unconscious of the cost in life to the old pioneers whose unrecorded exertions smoothed the way, and many of whose bones rest in the unmarked sepulchres of the wilderness.

I am not concerned here to indulge or bore the reader with a recital of the personal adventures either in contest with savage men or animals which fell to my lot, as African literature is replete enough with stories of that kind from more facile pens than I can wield, but it may perhaps be permissible to mention that my wanderings of more than thirty years ago had already made me acquainted with immense tracts of the countries bounded to the north by the Zambesi, to the west by the Great Thirstland, and to the east by the Indian Ocean. Umsillegasse (Mossilikatze of the Boers) had settled down in the territories now annexed by the Chartered Company of Mr. Rhodes and conquered all the neighbouring tribes with

Zulu troops, invincible by any less powerful
opponents than the white invader. Varied by an
occasional visit to England, and other parts of the
world, the greater portion of half a century has
been passed by me under canvas on African soil
with unusual immunity from the endemic diseases
prevalent in so many parts of the Dark Continent
or being once laid up from any other cause than
an occasional fracture or strain. Within the last
five years, however, a wandering life has been
succeeded by retirement in the sleepy hollow of
a Colonial village, in view of the educational
advantages for a young family growing up around
me. In such places life undergoes a process of
oxidation, and the only excitements indulged in
by the inhabitants apparently consist of a chronic
round of religious dissipation, either in corybantic
or other forms which I fail to appreciate at their
possible value, but in the midst of which fate seems
to have ordained me to grasp the fag end of a
long life.

CHAPTER III.

GAME AND SPORT IN SOUTH AFRICA.

VISITORS to the Cape and Natal Colonies consisting for the most part of town dwellers with but little of the cacoæthes venandi in their disposition, and confining their travelling operations to the few but much frequented lines of rail and road between the coast and the great mining centres, would, no doubt, if answering an enquiry as to the prospects of shooting in these countries, honestly reply that the prospects were anything but bright. But no country in any comfortably accessible part of the world is better supplied with greater variety of game animals and birds than are many vast tracts within Colonial limits; nowhere may good sport be more freely indulged at a minimum of expense or fewer vexatious restrictions.

There are laws restricting the pursuit of game within certain times and seasons, according to the shillings, has to be procured, but as a rule, in answer to a civil request, few are churlish enough to refuse permission to shoot on their properties.

Few of the Africander population care much about shooting anything, but now and then an antelope if an easy pot shot is available; but to work for feathered game on foot in English fashion has no sufficient attraction. Once outside a radius of a few miles from the larger towns shooting is practically free, and information as to the best kinds of game specified; a licence, costing ten nature of various localities, and the habits of the localities for sport easily obtainable. Even within eighty or one hundred miles of Cape Town these remarks apply, and very fair bags of francolin, of two varieties, and of a bustard, called koorhaam, are to be made in many localities; nor are the smaller antelopes, such as grysbock, steinbuck, and "duiker" by any means scarce on the more level parts of the country, and wildfowl of various sorts are a certain find in sufficient numbers in suitable places.

On the lower slopes of the mountains the buck antelopes (which weigh about 60 lb., clean) are mostly to be found in small troops of from three or four to a dozen or so, but as they usually frequent open ground devoid of bush they must be stalked, and a good rifle is the weapon to carry.

Higher up among the precipitous rocks near the summits the African chamois (klipspringer) is always to be found, and being but seldom disturbed is easily approachable.

This very beautiful little antelope. is a miracle of activity, and the soles of its hoofs being more like indiarubber than horn in texture, it is able to poise itself safely on rocky pinnacles which would only seem to afford sufficient foothold for a bird. This antelope, when clean, weighs from 28 lb. to 32 lb., if in good condition. Its sharp little horns are about five inches long, and its coat is composed of even, quill-like hair about two inches in length, of a grayish colour with a yellowish tinge. This hair is easily detached from the skin by a very slight pull when the animal is freshly killed, and makes the very best stuffing for saddles, as it never packs or felts from the effects of pressure or perspiration, and, indeed, acts as efficient ventilation, thus preventing that tendency to sore backs so prevalent in all warm climates.

To any one with a taste for the labours and risks

of Alpine climbing klipspringer shooting ought to be a very attractive sport, notwithstanding the absence of snow generally, and the almost certain prevalence of fine open weather, in which it is rather pleasurable to sleep—"al fresco" if necessary.

In the rough mountain ravines leopards are now and again to be shot, especially where the large ursine baboons are numerous. Only two days previous to penning this a fine one was killed on a mountain close to the village I dwell in, which, as the crow flies, is about ninety miles from Cape Town. In the George district, and in the jungly country near the coast of the East Province, bush-bucks abound, but, unless "driven," are difficult to find or get a shot at.

In any marshy locality, where the water is fresh, good bags of snipe of three varieties may be made. Of these the common European sort is the most plentiful, but at certain seasons a good many couple of the "great snipe" are to be had, and in low warm marshes the painted snipe is common enough.

Hares are plentiful in places, and of the two varieties, the largest, which often weighs nine or ten pounds, is seldom found far from a good supply of running water; the smaller and more common kind very little exceeds an English wild rabbit in size. Both sorts are indifferent for table use.

In the northern parts of the Colony and in Griqualand West a few large bustards, called locally "pauws," are occasionally seen, and afford sport for the bullet. Springbucks are also to be had in those districts, and are still to be found in troops of a hundred, or more, in suitable places, i.e. vast bare plains, where they are quite unstalkable, and must be ridden into, or driven, when a, to me very unsatisfactory, random shot into the brown is often obtained.

Boers are very fond of springbuck shooting, as the majority of them are very poor shots at single objects unless they get a rest for the gun. It is true that by dint of an unlimited expenditure of ammunition they certainly destroy a great deal of game. In the year 1879 I hunted for two months in company with some Boers who made game shooting their business and were considered crack shots. Out of curiosity I kept an account of the number of shots they fired; the result was that every head of game bagged cost them thirty-two shots on an average. All the same they loaded up their waggons with hides, etc. I have met three Boers only who. would be considered really good game shots by the average English sportsman, and I have hunted with Boers many times.

Francolin shooting very much resembles sport on a grouse moor, and the birds are of the same size, but I think the former are, if anything, quicker on the wing than grouse. The largest bag of francolin I ever made in one day amounted to thirty-four brace. This was in the Graff Reinet district. My reason for shooting so many was that a large supply was wanted for commissariat purposes; otherwise I have always abstained from possible slaughter except as a matter of sheer business in the case of ivory, rhino horns, valuable hides, and so on.

A few specimens of almost all kinds of African big game, except giraffes, still exist in protected districts within Colonial limits, but they cannot be considered as objects of sport now, and no sportsman under the rank of a Royal, or perhaps a Serene, Highness should ever even wish to kill any of these survivors. These Colonies are hardly suitable hunting grounds for people addicted to the slaughter of semi-tame pheasants at hot corners, or even of deer enclosed within wire fences, but quite up to the mark aspired to by the real hard-working sportsman of reasonably developed destructive instincts, and it would be hard to find a better field than South Africa for the exertions of such men if properly equipped and capable of enjoying gipsy life in a splendid climate. For a man fond of hunting with hounds, exclusive, I mean, of the mere swelldom involved in the " get-up," I can fancy no sport to surpass that which could be obtained in South Africa with about five couple of staunch hounds of good speed and exceptional staying powers; a steinbuck or " duiker" as the quarry, and I speak from the experience of a few enjoyable runs of the kind in "auld lang syne."

In England it is indeed a very beautiful sight to witness the meet of a pack of hounds of twenty or more couple, but for the mere purpose of hunting, many dogs are superfluous, and tend rather to riot and the multiplication of checks than to successful sport. Fashion in this respect is probably irresistible, but that it is necessary to use such exuberant power to kill a miserable little fox, or even a deer, is more than questionable. Now both the antelopes I have mentioned are very superior to any fox, or deer, in speed and staying powers, and not seldom run horses and hounds to a standstill, which could not be evaded by the participations in pursuit of any number of hounds, however good. On the other hand, kills are often effected by a small good pack, but never, as far as my experience goes, without a long and severe run. In such a country as this, not being almost exclusively occupied in fencing, opening gates, galloping into and out of deep blind lanes, and so forth, as in England, hunting pur et simple can be thoroughly enjoyed when attainable, which, however, is too seldom the case. Strange to say, in such an arid climate scent is generally good, except in very hot noontide, by which time it is advisable to be getting home to breakfast.

For shooting purposes a good, strong, acclimatised pointer is the best kind of dog, if a man is content with an imperfectly educated animal not difficult to pick up at a moderate figure. For two men bound on a shooting trip in the regions I have indicated, a light spring waggon with, say, eight good mules should be procured. A suitable waggon affording comfortable sleeping quarters and plenty of space wherein to stow impedimenta, need not cost more than £40 secondhand, and is often to be got for much less. Good mules cost about £10 each in the Cape districts, and at the end of, say, a six months' trip the whole equipage would realise within a trifle of the price paid for it if sold further up the country. Meanwhile, no hotel expenses need be incurred. Almost every coloured boy of from fourteen to any age can drive six in hand well, and such hands are procurable for from £1 to £1 10s. a month, with food thrown in, of course. Two such boys should be taken— one to look after cattle and saddle horses, and the other drive, cook, and do all kinds of odd jobs. When extra help is temporarily required, it is generally to be had at the cost of a few shillings.

In some of the north-west parts of the Colony and in Griqualand West large bags of sand-grouse are to be made in the proper season.

The fishing to be had in South Africa is poor indeed as regards the eatable qualities of the spoil, which is usually either very coarse or flavourless and bony. One fairly good fish of the perch tribe is occasionally to be had, and, for anything I know to the contrary, is the only exception to the general rule; but then, I am bound to add, my piscatorial tastes are but feebly developed.

But it is time to offer a few remarks on the sport to be obtained at no great distances from Colonial limits, or at all events now easily accessible. In the settled parts of the Transvaal all kinds of game are very scarce. If desirous of getting a few specimens of the large class, the only reliable localities must be sought in or near the Lebombo boundary and along the line which marches with the Gaza country towards the lower waters of the Limpopo. Here a few elephants still roam restlessly, a rhino may be shot, and giraffes are not difficult to be found, as well as a few buffaloes and, in suitable places, hippos. Lions are also fairly represented, but owing to long grass and dense bush are difficult to find. Elands are not quite extinct, and fair numbers of koodoos, sable antelopes, brindled gnus, quaggas, road antelopes, waterbucks, hartebeestes, palla, bushbucks, ostriches, reitbucks, and wart-hogs inhabit the veldt here and there. The drawbacks in these parts are great mortality among horses at all times (exclusive of perhaps a few weeks in June and

July), occasional patches of the deadly tsetse fly, various and severe and endemic cattle diseases, and, lastly, the presence of severe African fever except during the months of from June to October, during which period, however, there is no certainty of immunity from an attack.

Another trip from Cape Town to Beira by steamship is now easily practicable, and all kinds of big game still abound within moderate distances of the port. Waggon travelling is unavailable there, as draught animals all speedily succumb to the effects of tsetse bites, and for the same reason all hunting must be done on foot. Impedimenta are usually carried by natives, who, however, are now only more or less reliable, but perhaps a light cart drawn by six donkeys (to be imported from the Colony) might be advantageously employed for the transport of a limited amount of baggage for a trip not exceeding about six weeks in duration, as donkeys usually live for that space, or a little longer, in a tsetse country, although all die from the effects of the poison eventually. In this part of the world an attack of fever is by no means uncommon at any season, but is most imminent in acute form from November to June, inclusive.

In the Chartered Company's territories all species of African game animals are represented here and there, and sometimes good sport is to be had, under certain restrictions as to seasons and amount of slaughter. Those parts of the country consisting for the most part of highland plateaux are mostly healthy enough for men, but horses are decimated by the African distemper. Near the Zambesi the country is always feverish, and game not very abundant now.

A trip in the Great Thirst Land of the Kalliharri I have found pleasurable enough, given a good crop of the indigenous watermelon, which is uncertain, or an unusually good rainfall. This desert is exceptionally healthy for man and beast at all seasons, and the pasturage is the very best to be found in Africa. Here, in various parts, giraffe and eland are to be got, the stately gembuck is often plentiful, and brindled gnus, hartebeestes, and springbuck are denizens of these dry lands. Of running water there is none, and in other forms that element is rare, but by good management, and under experienced guidance, a very pleasant time may be spent in the Kalliharri and good sport obtained. The smaller game to be always found consist of steinbucks and duikers, bustards (both large and small), innumerable sand-grouse near pools, and, when the hollows have been converted into lakelets by a heavy fall of rain, these are covered with all kinds of wildfowl, and fine sport is obtainable. Francolin are unknown in or near the Kalliharri. An occasional lion is not uncommon, and leopards are in some places exceptionally numerous and aggressive. In the absence of surface waters these carnivora satisfy thirst by absorbing wild watermelons, which are always obtainable in some parts of this vast tract of country. Immense surfaces of the desert are covered with high sand dunes, the sides of which are grassy and thinly sprinkled over with bush, and even large timber trees are not rare. In such localities first-rate stalking sport is more practicable than in any other part of Africa I am acquainted with. And now it occurs to me that in my enumeration of African game birds I omitted to mention guineafowl, which are in some places, especially on the Limpopo, very numerous, but give better results in the pot than as objects of sport, as they are desperate runners, and difficult of approach except when treed by a dog. On the subject of personal adventures I feel disinclined to write, as they have very generally resembled those so graphically treated by Mr. Selous and others of the South African guild of hunters and pioneers.

THE END OF AN ADVENTURE.

CHAPTER IV.

LIONS.

IT has been suggested to me that a few additional remarks on some of the characteristics of lions, and of the hunting of them, might be acceptable to brother sportsmen, and it occurs to me that I can hardly do better than commence by giving some account of the facts and inferences with which a long intimacy with the leonine family has stored my memory.

It has, I have noticed, become the fashion of many modern sportsmen, who have had the good fortune to kill a few lions with impunity, to shower abusive and contemptuous epithets on the head of this very prominent member of the upper circles of animal society; just as in former times so many absurd stories of his magnanimity and courage were current and credited. The fact remains that he is pre-eminently a very crafty beast; when circumstances warrant it a very reckless and dangerous one to deal with offensively, and I feel confident in stating this upon the strength of the evidence that between 1847 and the sixties. upwards of eighty casualties, many of them fatal and all very serious, occurred to white hunters, inhabiting chiefly the Marico district and its neighbourhood, solely attributed to the results of contests with this despot of the plains. Since then accidents of this kind have been rare, as the Boers have annihilated, for the sake, of their hides, the vast herds of ruminating game which had covered the bare plains of the Free State and Transvaal.

During the period alluded to not only had many lions fallen victims to " vile saltpetre " influence, but, their food supplies rapidly diminishing to a vanishing point, the surviving regal beasts betook themselves to safer quarters in the northern and eastern bushbelt, where it is very difficult to find them, and more so to get a fair shot. Within a short time the lions will disappear entirely in the absence of adequate food supplies, as, what between rifles and rinderpest, little game of any suitable kind will exist. In my early hunting days, in the bush country of the lower part of the Marico River, and all along the course of the Limpopo and its tributaries, lions in considerable numbers existed and made night hideous with their incessant roaring. It was the same in the bush country along the courses of Oliphant's River and its affluents, but by day they were seldom visible, and it was rather rare to bag one. On the High Veldt, or open plains, I have mentioned it was hardly possible to ride about in likely places for an hour or so without seeing several lions either singly or in family groups more or less numerous. Whilst rumbling along the wheel tracks which then did duty as roads, the waggon often disturbed their siestas in the sun, when they would generally make off at a leisurely walk, but if very replete with food would sometimes refuse to move, and oblige the traveller to make a détour to avoid collision.

On such occasions to fire at them was to run the risk of causing the emission of angry growls, and a consequent panic among the draught oxen, resulting most likely in a bolt and a general smash-up. As a rule the lions escaped scathless. In such cases single lions were generally more apt to become aggressive than when met with in a troop, and I well remember that an acquaintance of mine, by name Cornelius Botha, while travelling with another man in a cart near Pretoria, which was then a very tiny village, had his pair of horses killed by a lion while leisurely ascending the bank of Pinaar's River after fording it. In this case the pair had only one M.L. single-barrel gun with them, and it refused to do more than explode several caps, otherwise the lion could have been easily killed as he was deliberately breakfasting on one of the horses, which was still attached to the cart by the harness. This sort of thing lasted for half an hour or so, and whenever the occupants of the cart moved an ominous growl warned them to remain stationary. After a time a waggon came up, and while fording the river the tremendous Boer whip cracked so loudly that the lion retired into a heavy reed bed hard by, and thus escaped being penalised for felony. On this occasion the brute had ensconced himself behind a low bush close to the road, in waiting, evidently, for anything or anybody of appetising appearance passing by, and he omitted the usual spring by which he mostly brings down a quarry, and merely stepped out near enough to throw a paw over the withers of the near-side horse and pulled it over, finishing the operation with a few bites through the neck of the victim. Meanwhile the off-horse had got mixed up with the harness and had fallen, failing to regain his feet before the lion had him by the throat in a fatal grip.

The new arrivals, after clearing the road of the dead horses, attached Botha's cart to the waggon, and towed it and its belongings to Waterberg, whither he was bound on official business, I believe. The whole of that road between Pretoria and Zoutpansberg was then infested by a very daring lot of lions, and one man-eater had his habitat a few miles to the north of the Waterberg settlement. He killed at least nine white travellers, not to mention a lot of Kaffirs, previous to his execution by special commands. These lions did their evil deeds mostly in broad daylight, and during a journey along that road with Zoutpansberg as my objective, shortly after Botha's adventure, three of them refused to allow my people to fetch water from a little spring west of the road, and I had to knock over one of the trio before getting a supply. The other two disappeared after sniffing at their dead friend and while I was reloading my single muzzle-loading duck gun, which

I had got altered to percussion before leaving England. As it weighed fourteen pounds, it was not ideally handy on horseback, but I shot an immense quantity of game with it, ranging from elephants to the small steinbuck antelope, and lost very few animals wounded by its large spherical bullet, which it shot accurately at quite outside distances.

Lions are very skilful strategists, and do not as a rule show much dangerous fight unless in a well-selected position. When attacked on rough stony ground they are very reluctant to charge and thus endanger the integrity of their claws, upon which they are in a great measure dependent for a livelihood; but when on the open alluvial plains, although they generally try to elude pursuit by a sulky retreat, if pressed upon too rudely they soon become very ugly customers to deal with, and straight powder becomes an essential element on the hunter's side.

I will now allude more especially to the Boer method of lion hunting, when it is customary to assemble as many men as possible (generally twenty or so) and ride on the quest in more or less close order. When a view of the game is obtained, if he declines to move, the horsemen ride towards him in a body and dismount at about one hundred yards, tie their horses' heads together, with rumps towards the lion, and one or two of the men at a time fire from the flanks of the body of horses at any exposed part of the quarry, which is generally very small, as lions instinctively select any little depressions they may come across to lie down in, from which they can see without exposing themselves to be clearly viewed, or in default. of a hollow any good-sized bunch of herbage serves their purpose. If the lion, on becoming aware of the advance of his enemies, beats a retreat he never puts on much steam, and a couple of the best mounted Boers gallop along at a safe distance from each of his flanks, but a little ahead of him if possible; then the lion usually drops flat into the first available hollow, and the main body of horsemen collect together and proceed to action in the before-mentioned manner.

I have been a spectator of this sort of hunting several times, but always remained mounted, and never cared to fire a shot. On these occasions very poor shooting is generally the order of the day, and if the lion is peppered ineffectually for any length of time he often charges into the brown of his assailants effectively. I once witnessed a performance of the kind in which three horses got fearfully torn up, and one young Boer had his foot seriously crushed by the hoof of a panic-stricken horse.

I have known only four Boer hunters who ever venture a conflict with lions when on foot, or not well within reach of a horse. Personally, my impression is that the safest and most effectual method of lion hunting is alone, with a gun-bearer carrying a spare weapon, or at most with one trusty fellow hunter, and I have never had occasion to complain, as I have heard many do, of the behaviour of a native attendant, if isolated from companions of his own race. And here I may remark that although I have been in many tight corners when hunting lions I have never been mauled, nor has any casualty befallen any of my "boys" on these occasions.

And now perhaps it may be well briefly to describe the first rather serious trying incident I experienced, although previously several lions had fallen to my gun in the usual order of such events. On the occasion about to be mentioned my camp was pitched on a game-covered plain in the (now) Orange Free State, not far from Kaffir River. A nice pool of rainwater was close at hand; and, at some few hundred yards off, a low rocky ridge clotted with thorn clumps here and there bounded the view to the north. Hundreds of black gnus were capering about in all directions; long columns of blesbucks occasionally swept by in orderly array; quaggas in smaller troops were busily cropping the dewy grass of the early morning; and thousands of springbucks varied the ever shifting scene of animal life visible from the camp. It is safe to say that no future traveller will ever view the like, as not only was the vast plain beautifully green in consequence of late heavy rains, but not a tree or a bush intervened to obstruct the sight of the animated panorama till the eye was fatigued by peering into the distance.

The time I allude to was the month of May, 1853, and a young Englishman, who was a taxidermist in my employ, and myself were sitting by the fire enjoying an early cup of coffee and a chat, when the cackling of a large troop of guinea-fowl from the stony ridge attracted our attention and promised a welcome change of diet, everybody

having become weary of the dry antelope meat we
had so long fed on. My companion had work in
hand—of which fact I was rather glad, as he was
about the worst shot in South Africa, albeit one
of the pluckiest fellows I have met. So I started
alone for the " randt " before mentioned, taking a
favourite little 16 double gun (by Beckwith, of
Snow Hill, London), with 26-inch barrels, loaded
with No. 5 shot, and some spare ammunition, inclusive of a few bullets, to be in a position to
defend myself from molestation in case of need,
as the lions had been very noisy all night.

Before getting to the stony ridge, I could see
the guineafowl were busily making rapid tracks
towards the summit, and just as I gained it were
disappearing down the other side, as the top of
the ridge was only about forty yards wide.
Stumbling along in pursuit, suddenly I trod on
something soft, and instinctively took a good spring
off it. Before I could look round a fearful growling became audible, and two lion cubs, about the
size of an ordinary sporting spaniel, became
visible, evidently in a fury at being so roughly
disturbed. Not wishing to kill them, I was just
about to signal for assistance to the camp, with

a view to catch them, when I caught a glimpse of a lioness rapidly but cautiously making for me.

There was no time to put bullets in the gun, and I swiftly decided to stand perfectly still till it became clear that the lioness meant to seize me, and as a last chance then to send a charge of shot at her head, in the hope of blinding her at least. In a few moments the brute was within four yards or so of me, growling and showing her teeth ominously. But she halted, so I decided to remain still, lest any movement should indicate hostile intentions on my part, and thus invite an attack. The cubs now joined their dam, and she just looked down at them for a moment, but maintained a menacing attitude for some time, then turned slowly round, and, followed by the cubs, made for a huge boulder about twenty yards distant, and passing round it, lay down on the other side, as I could see by the black tail tuft which protruded beyond the edge of the rock.

This boulder was about twelve feet high, and of proportionate diameter, but appeared fairly climbable for stockinged feet from my standpoint, so I hastily rammed down two bullets on the top of the shot charge, kicked off my shoes, stuck the little gun through my belt at the back, and, creeping stealthily, soon reached the big round top of the stone, and, peering over, saw the lioness close under me, on her belly, in form for a spring, and with her head well up, evidently in a mood to resent any further molestation. Her youngsters were pottering about, no doubt staring with great yellow eyes in the same direction as their dam, but, like her, evidently unaware of my position. It goes without saying that I took every possible care to get my gun into firing position without disturbing the trio, and then immediately let drive at the lioness, aiming between the shoulders. The combined charge of shot and ball rolled her over at once, and not only smashed the backbone, but made a terrible mess of the contents of her chest. By this time, and before quitting my position of vantage, my companion and some of the " boys," having heard the row at the waggon, were coming up, after arming themselves, some with guns, and others with assegais; so the cubs were soon caught at the expense of a few bites and scratches, and, together with the skin of the slain, carried into camp.

These cubs were male and female, and became

inhabitants of a rough but strong cage of bush scrub, in which they dwelt for some months, and grew before reaching Port Elizabeth to the size of large mastiffs. There they were bought by an American skipper, and realised fifty guineas.

The last time I came into unpleasant contact with a lion occurred some eight years ago in the Setabi country, Zoutpansberg district, when returning from a very poor hunting trip, during which I had lost a number of trek oxen, my only horse, and five donkeys from local disease. All the rest looked half starved, although the whole country was covered with grass varying from a foot to seven feet high. Some Boer hunters we met with had been even more unfortunate in these respects; moreover, several of their number were down with fever, and one died. His grave I helped to dig, and noticed that the soil, although perfectly dry, emitted a vile smell when disturbed.

There was a fair enough show of game, consisting of a few elephants, rhinoceros, buffaloes, sable antelopes, ostriches, pallahs, and others of smaller note. Giraffes, too, abounded, and the Boers massacred twenty-four in one day, wasting most of the meat of course, as few or no natives inhabit this pestiferous country to take advantage of the reckless and cruel slaughter these hunters invariably commit from the mere love of bloodshed —especially that which can be effected with safety.

And at the expense of a little further digression I may mention that giraffe meat and marrow, when obtained from any but the old bulls, would be a treat to an alderman even after a rib-distending dose of turtle soup. Well, when we were at the Setabi drift (or ford), and about to leave the game country, a camp was pitched for a rest and some perch fishing. The "boys" got leave for a day's hunt, which resulted in the death of a fat quagga—to their intense delight. Unfortunately I lent them my guns, and was quietly reading in the waggon, when a young English Africander who was travelling in our company, and had gone out with two Boers before I awoke, brought in the news that they had wounded a lion not half a mile off, which, with his mate, they had found feeding on a captured Sassabi antelope, begging me at the same time to help them to kill him if possible.

Having loaned a very dilapidated Martini and a few cartridges, I mounted my friend's horse, and he walked alongside. Thoughtlessly enough I put the cartridges into a pouch attached to the saddle, as the " boys " were absent with my bandolier. Off we went, soon reaching up with the two Boers, who were sitting waiting for us with bridles in hand and smoking like young furnaces. It appeared that my young friend, who was chock full of pluck, could not persuade his companions to approach the lions within less than three hundred yards; then they insisted on firing, with the result that one lion was hit, and both beat a retreat, loudly protesting against the assault and battery. ·

Getting on the spoor, we followed it, and shortly sighted one lion trotting away straight ahead, and immediately gave chase, but soon lost him in a deep nullah full of savage thorns and creepers which in the local patois are called monkey ropes. The country was only here and there studded with a few bushes, and the grass was short, but we had evidently left the wounded or dead lion in the rear, so the horses were turned, and the Boers led by some fifty yards or so at a smart walk, and, crossing a little sandy nullah, were invisible in the bush on the other side when we crossed it.

We had hardly done this, when a fine yellow-maned lion emerged from behind a large tree, cleared the nullah at a bound, and laid down seven paces (as we found afterwards) in front of my horse, who became fractious, turned tail, bucked me off, and bolted, when I was attempting to dismount to join my friend, who stood like a rock, but fortunately refrained from firing at my request, as I by no means relied on his shooting powers, although he was armed with an excellent 8-bore rifle which I had sold him.

I was hors de combat, my Martini having opened and thrown out the cartridge when I fell. As it was absolutely necessary to recover this cartridge, I crept forward in unpleasant proximity to the lion, but got it. My friend covered me well during this operation, and indeed the lion was looking at the Boers, who had heard the row and galloped to a large tree two hundred yards off, whence they opened fire and duly missed several shots, thus giving us an opportunity of reaching with impunity a mound hard by, affording a clear shot at thirty paces. Having promised the shot to my companion—who had never before seen a wild lion—he sat down, and, as the lion was now end on, fired at the nose, which, to my astonishment, he hit. The ball, after blowing the brain to atoms, smashed the lower neck bones and a couple of feet of the backbone, finally lodging in the loins, and the lion died without even a visible convulsive motion. On examination we found that the first hit had merely ripped up the skin of the left thigh for a few inches and scarcely drawn a drop of blood.

This lion was just full grown and in fine condition, and weighed by estimation about four hundred pounds. I sent the skin and skull as a present to a gentleman in Scotland. During the trip these were the only lions I saw, although we often enough heard them both in the night and early morning. Shortly after this rumpus we came into the camp of a young English transport rider named Daniels, who had brought loads to Barberton Mine, and had gone down into the plains along the Oliphant's River to rest and recruit his wearied oxen. Here a lion killed one of his beasts, and Daniels, taking his Martini and a Boer, the animal was soon found and wounded by a shot fired by Daniels, who, after inserting another cartridge, followed up the wounded beast and found him lying in some grass behind a small bush. Being uncertain whether the lion was dead or not, he asked his Boer friend to throw a stone at him, and this brought on a charge at once. Daniels' rifle missed fire, and he dropped it and seized the lion by the ears and surrounding mane, and, being a very powerful young fellow, held him for some little time. This, however, could not last, and soon Daniels was thrown down and bitten severely in the knee and calf of his leg—after which the lion left him.

Had the Boer been anything better than a sorry cur, he could easily have killed the lion, or tried to do so, before any serious damage was done, but the fellow got a panic, and made at tip-top speed for a Boer waggon camp a mile or so distant, with his loaded gun in his hand. Here, upon hearing the story, six or seven Boers mounted, and after a while killed the lion, and carried Daniels to his tent, where we found him reduced to a skeleton, and evidently crippled for life.

Of course we camped at once and did what was possible for the poor fellow, despatching a messenger to Barberton asking for help, and a few days afterwards some Kaffirs appeared with a stretcher and carried the sufferer to the mine, where he got medical assistance. Whether he lived or died I never heard.

What with the long grass, full of hidden boulders, and of the unusually good supplies of water, the greater part of the country near the Lebombo is very difficult, and more or less dangerous to hunt. Fresh " spoor " is always to be seen, but all kinds of game know well how to avail themselves of cover, and but few shots are obtainable. As a wholly impenetrable jungle, not to mention tsetse-fly, extends from the eastern side of the range at intervals down to the coast, all kinds of game will find in these parts secure sanctuary for an indefinite but most probably long time.

Man-eating lions were never numerous in South Africa, but they existed, and a Kaffir of mine, by name Aaron, was killed by one while washing clothes, against my positive orders, in the Marico River; I think in 1864. We had been warned of the lion's probable presence near at hand by some Kaffirs, whose kraal was not far from the waggons, who had lost seven of their number from his attacks within a short time. This was indeed a cunning old brute, as he took up poor Aaron, after killing him, and carried him off to a distance, and although we pursued him and found pieces of the victim's clothes along the spoor for more than a mile, we eventually lost all trace of the murderer, owing to the very thick bush and the abundance of other lion spoor, as well as that of much other game quite fresh. Returning some months afterwards, I was glad to find that the Kaffirs had killed him by planting several assegais in a slanting direction in the ground and placing a dog as bait. To get at this he was obliged to jump a low fence just in front of the sharp blades, two of which went right through him as he landed from jumping the fence the same night the trap was laid. Notwithstanding this, he killed the dog, and got some fifty yards away from the kraal before he fell dead with the dog still in his mouth, and was so found by the Kaffirs next morning.

My losses from leonine depredations have been small, and included one Kaffir, one horse and four oxen in all. Nevertheless, I consider lions very dangerous brutes under treatment with gunpowder, in spite of all that has been lately written about their insignificance and cowardice. I fancy Dr.

Livingstone started the idea I advert to, although he had one arm completely smashed by a lion bite, and he even went so far as to write that the being mauled by an animal of the kind was by no means a very unpleasant sensation. Well, the Doctor was certainly one of the most intrepid of men, but I have heard him say that he was a very poor shot, and generally deficient in sporting proclivities.

CHAPTER V.

WITH rapid and relatively cheap travel, English sportsmen have opportunities to visit countries where good sport offers. In spite of the available information on the subject of foreign sport, I have observed that men intending to obtain it usually encumber themselves with batteries as expensive as they are superfluous.

In all wild countries it may be taken for granted that transport is more or less difficult, imperfect, and expensive, and the obligation to be constantly on the alert to watch over the safety of a costly battery soon becomes intolerable, and a waste of energy in a profitless direction. I venture, therefore, by virtue of my experience of half a century, in many lands, but chiefly in Africa, to offer some items of advice to brother sportsmen who contemplate " going foreign." Having used nearly every kind of weapon of portable dimensions from the flint-and-steel days up to 1894, perhaps I may lay a claim to some practical knowledge of the subject. Previous to giving an opinion on the arms which seem to me most efficient, a few remarks on those which appear to me to be unnecessary or inefficient may not be misplaced.

As to weapons, I have found a strong plain 16-bore, one barrel cylinder and the other modified choke, twenty-four inches long, best in every way. The cylinder barrel of any well-bored double gun with a suitable quantity of metal, if fitted with a leaf folding-sight on the rib, and loaded with a thick soft wad below a hardened spherical bullet, will, if the bullet is a close but not tight fit, shoot accurately enough to hit anything of or about the size of a rabbit at one hundred yards or there-abouts. I have a gun of the size mentioned which weighs six and a quarter pounds, and I find it is as serviceable as any ordinary gun of 12-bore, and very handy. I don't think there is practically much difference in the killing powers of guns of from twelve to twenty bore, unless the larger bore is heavy enough to be used with four drams of powder and one and a half ounce of shot. Indeed, with a 28-bore I have killed satisfactorily small antelopes, geese, and wildfowl, besides several large bustards, with shot of suitable size (No. 1 for choice), but as it was an extra stout little weapon, I used a powder charge of two drams of C. and H. No. 4 powder in it, and the same measure of shot.

It is as well for each man to have a spare gun on an African trip, to provide for contingencies. A good sightly double gun can be procured from any Birmingham maker for from £10 to £12, and an equally efficient but plainer one for £7 10s. (non-ejectors, of course), and I really cannot see the use of paying London gunmakers high prices for their wares.

Personally, for general use even with ball, I prefer a suitable cylinder smooth bore for all kinds of game, elephants to snipe inclusive; but I have also shot with all kinds of rifles, and have a decided preference for the smooth oval bored weapons on Mr. C. Lancaster's principle, which are quite as accurate at sporting distances as grooved rifles, retain their shooting qualities indefinitely, foul and recoil very little, and are especially easy to clean, besides being available for use with shot when expedient. The new much-bepraised ·303 rifle is, for its size, a very powerful weapon, with indeed superfluous powers of range and penetration, for sporting purposes; it soon goes off its shooting under stress of work and cleaning, its unique advantage consisting of the lightness of its ammunition.

For foreign use, especially in hot, dry climates, it is very important to select such as are chambered for what gunmakers call the straight taper cartridge case, as these never jam, can be reloaded an indefinite number of times without resizing, and thus obviate the portage of a set of implements easily mislaid or lost, or, if resizing is repudiated as a nuisance, the necessity of carrying about a very cumbersome amount of cartridges. I have found that one hundred straight cartridge cases can be reloaded fifteen times at least without resizing, but that bottle-necked ones must be put through that process after each shot or thrown away; another objection to them is that if made in an extreme form—such as that of the regulation cartridge for the Martini—recoil is very much increased.

Soldiers both in the Soudan and Boer wars very justly complained of these vagaries, but

attributed them to effects caused by the nature of
the action, and not to those incidental to the faulty
form of the chamber and the cartridge case, which
was, however, a mistaken idea. Most probably
a gunmaker with a very keen eye to the sale of
cartridges and implements introduced these bottle-
necked abominations. That department of the
Government entrusted with the selection of the
small-arms and ammunition for military equipment
has, from all time within living memory, been
afflicted with a chronic affection for the time-
honoured practice of the art of "how not to do
things" in accordance with the rules of common-
sense. When old "Brown Bess" was the weapon
of the infantry, although the barrel was of excellent
form, material, and make, the lock was at least of
twice the needful weight, carefully fitted with an
impossible trigger, and the stock so shaped as
to be quite certain to inflict a very severe blow
on the cheekbone of any soldier with nerve enough
to try to take aim when firing. The bore of this
obsolete weapon was eleven, and it was charged
with four and a half drams of powder behind a
ball of fourteen, no less, that is, than three sizes
too small, the consequences of which were that,

owing to the needless excess of windage, the ballistic energy of, at most, two and a half drams of powder was applicable to propulsion of the bullet, and the rush of the gases of the rest of the powder past the projectile ensured all possible inaccuracy and a very short range. I had the curiosity to try one of these obsolete weapons with the service cartridge, and the result was that it was just possible very occasionally to hit a rock, six feet by three, at one hundred yards. The same weapon fired from the shoulder, and reasonably loaded although clumsily sighted, and with the worst possible " come up " and " pull," would, at a hundred yards, put every bullet into a fifteen-inch bull; even at three hundred yards shot quite well enough to entitle it to rank as a very useful implement in military operations.

Mutatis mutandis the same appetite for inutilities is still rampant; our troops are now armed with a rifle whose life ends in infancy, not to mention numerous minor defects carefully elaborated to ensure inefficiency.

Owing to the vast improvements in modern rifles in the direction of increased powers of penetration and of low trajectory, the modern gunner is in a much better position than his predecessors, and in order to deal successfully with the biggest game animals it is no longer necessary to be encumbered with heavy large-bore rifles and the corresponding weight of ammunition. A rifle with 26-inch barrels ·577-bore, and 10lb. weight is quite efficient, and I have observed that elephants, rhinos, and other big game fall to the shots from ·450-bore rifles in the most satisfactory way. Nor is it necessary to charge a ·577-bore rifle with more than 4 or 4½ drams of powder—(black, or its equivalent in nitro)—or the ·450-bore with more than 85 grains. Personally, I prefer smaller charges for all purposes except elephant or rhino shooting. Moderate charges of powder give quite sufficient penetration, and are not so liable to cause a premature breaking-up of the projectile, while they minimise recoil, which is a fertile source of error, and in all respects undesirable. For all-round purpose an express rifle is an inefficient tool, although when a very fair shot can be obtained all soft-skinned animals may be killed with it. However, in the field it is very often necessary to fire raking shots at the stern of good-sized antelopes and gnus, and in that case the short express bullet fails to do more than inflict a large superficial wound, with which the poor animal usually escapes. On two occasions I have known an express bullet break up and fail to fracture the neckbone of antelopes at close quarters, one of which was a waterbuck weighing probably four hundred pounds, and the other a pallah of about one hundred and twenty-five pounds. Both the animals escaped, but were shot some days afterwards and examined. It was not impossible for both to have recovered from the effects of the express bullet after a prolonged period of suffering.

In wild countries like Africa, where the game is seldom within very short range, is extremely wary, active, and tenacious of life, and must be fired at in any position or left alone, the express projectile is worthless. Two double expresses, one by Purdey and the other by Holland and Holland, were tried by me in the field, but I found them useless except for very easy side shots when using the regular express projectile; with a solid one the performance of these rifles was excellent. Of all the different kinds of rifles I have tried in the field, I distinctly prefer the Lancaster oval smooth-bore. I never got one from the maker direct, but was fortunate enough to buy one of ·577-bore at an auction of a deceased officer's effects, which served me well for some seasons, but, tempted by a high bid, I at length parted with it regretfully. These rifles are not only accurate, but stand rough wear and tear and neglect much better than any grooved ones, which latter kind soon go off their best shooting unless kept in tip-top order; moreover, the oval bore, for obvious reasons, recoils less than a grooved one, and what fouling there is, which is very little, is evenly distributed over the smooth inside surface of the barrel, instead of packing in patches as is the case with all grooved rifles more or less. They are therefore much easier to clean. Barrels of sporting rifles need never exceed twenty-six inches in length, both on account of handiness and because short guns can be held much steadier during the aiming period, or in high winds, than long ones. To facilitate quick focussing of the sights, the stocks of all rifles should be much more bent than usual. A man of 5 ft. 10 in. cannot do his level best at quick or running shots with a bend of less than three inches. One turn of the rifling in twenty-six inches is ample for sporting weapons, as up to 1,000 yards, or more, such a " pitch " is quite sufficient to obviate any risk of the upsetting of the projectile. Any excess in the pitch of the rifling means increased recoil, fouling, and leading. To fire at game at distances in excess of two hundred and fifty yards is un-sportsmanlike, and tends to the infliction of much unnecessary cruelty. Indeed, after the exertion entailed by a gallop or a stalk, no man is fit enough to shoot with tolerable accuracy at more than point-blank distances, unless he by chance gets a rest before being obliged to fire. Where cost is of no importance, a first-rate double-barrel is the best and most reliable rifle yet invented ; if economy is an object, the Colt and Winchester repeaters are efficient weapons. As repeating rifles are made in wholesale fashion, a purchaser should be careful to subject such weapons to a good trial previous to acquisition, as although most of them shoot with strength and accuracy, I have met with some eminently unsatisfactory as regards accurate performance, although, to all appearance, of excellent material and workmanship. For all-round work, ball and shot guns of the Colindian or " Paradox " type are very satisfactory weapons, and if made as 12-bores heavy enough to carry a charge of from 4 to 4½ drams of powder easily, they will kill satisfactorily any and every kind of game animal. A battery consisting of a double rifle of 9½ lb. weight, and one of these ball-and-shot guns of 8 lb., is an efficient armament for use in any part of the world, and for any kind of game. And here I may remark that the modern craving for very light guns is carried to excess. It surely matters very little to any man of ordinary powers whether he carries a 12-bore of 7 lb. or a little more, or one of 5 lb.; and after all the heavier gun is the safer and more efficient. If weight must be reduced, it is better done by shortening the barrels than by a reduction of substance; or, better still, go in for smaller bores. Reverting to the subject of rifles, I would remark that nickel-coated projectiles are in no degree superior to those made of well-hardened lead, except when the pitch of the rifle is excessive and the bore smaller than ·450. When such arms are used, the coated bullet is absolutely necessary, as the enormous friction created by the propulsion of a long, slender bullet by means of 40 grains of powder through such tubes would melt or crush up an uncoated projectile. A great deal of discussion on the merits or otherwise of the ·303 rifle has taken place, and upon the whole it may be admitted that its merits as regards penetration and flat trajectory are undeniable; its accuracy is also uncontestable but limited in duration, as a few months' hard work is sufficient to wear out the rifling, and thus displace it at short date from the position of a weapon of precision. The easy portability of its ammunition is a great point in its favour as a military arm, or as one for the defensive purposes of exploring parties in wild countries where the means of transport are limited, as is usually the case, and where it would only exceptionally be used for special services of infrequent occurrence. The action of this rifle when made on magazine lines is decidedly clumsy, and not unlikely to get out of order under stress of work; and upon the whole, although for long shots in an open country it may be effective, it is hardly the right sort of weapon for the wandering sportsman. The difficulties in keeping such small bores in an efficiently clean state are accentuated in the case of the ·303 rifle by the extreme, and as it seems to me quite unnecessary, pitch of the rifling, which naturally retains and packs the fouling to an inordinate degree, difficult to overcome satisfactorily.

Upon the whole, this rifle is the very last weapon I should care to be armed with when in conflict with an African buffalo, or even an angry lion. A campaign can alone test its value as a military weapon. It would seem that extreme range and the flattest possible trajectory are only obtainable at the cost of destructive friction. Extreme range is a matter of no importance to the sportsman who, if well advised, will never find it pay to make a habit of firing at game distant more than two hundred and fifty yards, and as an actual fact will only occasionally kill much over one hundred and fifty yards, no matter what sort of rifle he uses. As regards penetration, any good rifle of ·577, ·500, or ·450 is quite up to requirements, and the same remark applies to smooth-bore guns of from 10- to 16-gauge loaded with hard, close-fitting spherical bullets, assuming the gun to be sufficiently solid to use with an effective charge of powder.

Some years ago, when specially bent on a buffalo hunt, my battery consisted of one M.L.

single . 8-bore rifle, by Daw, of Threadneedle Street, London, and a good strong smooth-bore double M.L. of 16-bore, by Osborne and Sons, Birmingham, the latter being fitted with a back sight and an ivory front sight. Shortly before reaching the buffalo ground, the trigger of the 8-bore was accidentally broken, and I had to rely on the little smooth-bore, with which, however, in a few days forty-three of these animals were brought to bag, very few indeed escaping which were hit, and several were knocked over by raking shots from behind. Moreover, three full-grown cow elephants fell, during the same trip, to bullets from the same gun, which improved the profit of the hunt by the value of about fifty pounds of ivory. On another occasion, when on an elephant hunt, I found a plain but specially built smooth 12-bore double, with 26-inch barrels, weighing about 9 lb., as effective as any weapon I ever handled when charged with 4½ drams of fine grain C.H. powder. Indeed, I was astonished at the penetrating powers of this gun, which on one occasion drove its hard spherical ball through the left side of one of the bones of the dorsal column of a huge bull elephant, cut the large artery beneath, and was extracted from the muscles of the heart. The elephant when he received the shot was crossing a deepish nullah, and I fired from the saddle, having pulled up at the edge of the steep descent at about twenty yards distant from the bull, which collapsed at once. On another occasion, with the same gun, I fired at the stern of a giraffe, striking her a few inches below the tail, and the ball traversed the body, passed up the long neck between skin and muscles, and fell out from under the ear when the Kaffirs were cutting off the head. No doubt a conical projectile from a rifle will penetrate a block of wood much deeper than a spherical ball can be made to do, but, judging from my own experience and published records on the subject, the conclusion come to is that in penetrating the elastic tissues of which animals are composed there is no very essential difference between the results achieved by either form of projectile at sporting distances.

Assuming that in many foreign countries a supply of cartridge cases is often difficult to obtain, and that to carry a very large quantity about is inconvenient, it behoves the "globe-trotter" to economise by reloading his cases instead of throwing them away, as probably he would do at home. Therefore an ejector gun is rather a nuisance than otherwise, especially when on horseback, and even on foot having to stoop to pick up the cases is troublesome. As regards cartridges, I prefer Kynoch's best paper ones to any I have tried, as I find that by omitting to " turn over," each case will serve for three shots, and sometimes for four. In fact, it is much better to omit the turning-over process whether the cases are required for re-loading or not, with a view to minimise recoil. To retain the wad over the shot in position, my plan is to pour over it a thin layer of melted paraffin wax as hot as possible, and cartridges so loaded may be carried, in a shoulder-bag or in the pocket, without damage for an indefinite time. In the absence of paraffin, gum will hold the shot wad in place, but if made too thick, or applied in excess, it sometimes damages the end of the case more or less, although not nearly so much as the turning-over process.

Spherical bullets are firmly retained in place by the use of a thin flannel patch ungreased.

Kynoch's best solid drawn cases for rifles will last for reloading at least fifteen times, as proved by experiment with a ·360 rifle charged with 40 grains of powder and a projectile of 200 grains. Upon the whole I have found it better to arm any of the "boys" who may have the wish or ability to shoot with plain single-barrel smooth-bore guns; with rifles they get into the habit of blazing away at all kinds of distances and waste ammunition: besides, by giving them a shot cartridge or two, they often bring in a toothsome bird for the larder when one is satiated with dry antelope meat. Such guns can be bought for about £5, and should be sighted for ball shooting up to one hundred yards.

A day's shooting now and then serves to stave off the sulks—a complaint to which all Africans are liable, especially when lying idly encamped for some time, with little to do but smoke in the intervals unemployed in gorging themselves to repletion.

In ordering guns or rifles for rough work, the maker should be persuaded to make the hand grip considerably thicker than usual, and it should be oval instead of round. Personally, I dislike a pistol hand grip, as being superfluous and tending to impede the hand when the left barrel is wanted in haste for a double shot.

A white foresight is the best for game shooting, but those made of ivory are very fragile and apt to shrink and fall out in dry, hot weather. Enamelled steel answers perfectly, and a touch of white paint, if chipped, is all that is required to repair it. Platina-lined back sights are a mistake in a sunny climate, as they glitter too much to allow of focussing the front sight distinctly, unless it is taken full, and thus are often the cause of a miss by firing too high. In fact, the back sight should be as black as possible, and if file-cut, so as to be always dull, so much the better. Assuming that game should not as a rule be fired at beyond two hundred yards, and that indeed very little is killed by even first-rate shots beyond one hundred and fifty, it is quite unnecessary to use any but the hundred yards' sight in the field. With a little practice—up to the distances mentioned—experience proves that the most effective shooting is made by taking as fine a sight as possible, and raising it a little above the spot usually aimed at when the object is out of the point-blank range of the weapon in use.

Distances are usually overestimated in the field,

and the attempt to adjust elevating sights to the
required nicety within the distances mentioned
will result in firing over the object in nine shots
out of ten. At all events, the very best game
shots in South Africa whom I have known have
found it better to restrict themselves to the use
of a single standard sight for all shots within
sporting distances. In war, as a general rule,
soldiers should be discouraged from using the
elevating sights unless when pelting an enemy's
battery or any stationary post or object at
distances ascertainable by trial shots. Our
disaster at Majuba Hill would never have
occurred had no elevating sights been on the
rifles; simply because it is fair to conclude that
out of the thousands of shots fired by our men
when the enemy were within two hundred and
fifty yards, at least a score or so would have been
hits if the rifles had not been oversighted—and
in that case the Boers would not have persevered
in the attack, as they freely admit. On that sad
occasion all the rifles taken by the Boers were
found sighted either for four hundred or seven
hundred yards, and the bullets actually flew clean
over the horses which the Boers left between our

position and their camp, to facilitate the hasty retreat which they expected would be compulsory. The probability is that if our troops had been armed with the old " Brown Bess " the Boers would not have been able to take the position, as then at all events the bullets would not have passed over them, and many would necessarily have struck amongst the enemy. As it was, even if our men had confined their defence to throwing stones they would probably have put more than one assailant hors de combat, which was all they achieved by their rifles.

As a weapon of war the Martini was certainly in abstract qualities far superior to any earlier model, and no doubt the new ·303 rifle with which our troops are armed is, as long as it lasts, even better. Nevertheless, if our military authorities are allowed to persist in keeping their men innocent of the requisite knowledge of how to use it effectually, it will be a mere " dummy "— an indication only of the ascendency of the obstinate stupidity which is so obvious in all our military arrangements, except such as are intended for mere display. In spite of anything said on such subjects, it is, however, certain that nothing tending to teach our soldiers the efficient use of the weapons placed in their hands will be attempted until some fearful defeat in the field again occurs, attributable to the want of skill in shooting on the part of our soldiers, and attracts the attention of the press, and thus elicits an expression of irresistible public opinion. It never seems to be the duty of any of our Administrations to give any attention to those details upon which military efficiency in front of an enemy depends, and if the numerical condition of the army is satisfactory, and it is supplied with the best modern arms, the public is satisfied. The instruction of the soldier in his peculiar vocation is supposed to be a matter of course, and this state of things is probably destined to last until really responsible officers are appointed and allowed a free hand within reasonable limits.

It is, I think, conceded by most experienced military men that in future warfare success will mainly depend, as far as mere fighting is concerned, on the individual powers of the combative units of an army, or, in simpler words, on efficient rifle shooting. Assuming this to be a correct view of the case, it would seem as imperative as it is easy to endeavour to double the efficiency of every regiment by making every man at least a fair rough shot. At present most regiments probably contain a few men of exceptional skill as riflemen, and to these few all the prizes and credit are accorded—to the disgust of the unskilled majority, who find no encouragement to improve themselves. I am not concerned to offer any advice on the details bearing on reforms in the direction hinted at, but I trust that I may escape being condemned as presumptuous on the plea that my opinions have been formed wholly independent of any professional bias, and based upon facts of which all concerned are, or ought to be, cognisant.

CHAPTER VI.

THE GREAT THIRST LAND.

WITHIN the boundaries of British Bechuanaland
the immense tract of country known as the Kalliharri covers a space of at least five hundred and
fifty miles north and south by about four hundred
in breadth. Where surface waters in the form of
pools, wells, or springs exist on its south-west edge,
here and there a few white settlers live as stock
farmers; and small communities of Bastaards,
Kaffirs, Korannas, Hottentots, and wild bushmen
lead a semi-nomadic life dependent on their scanty
flocks and herds, eked out by the produce of an
occasional hunt.

No cultivation is attempted, as every drop of
water has to be economised for the use of the
people and their live stock, the numbers of which
are limited by the quantity of water available for
their use. The pasturage is far superior to any

THE MARKET PLACE, PRETORIA.

to be found elsewhere in South Africa, and some day, when the requisite means for tapping the subterranean supplies of water have been seriously and scientifically applied, this desert will probably supply more exportable produce in the form of wool, hides, and tallow than the whole of the Cape Colony, as the endemic diseases so fatal to the interests of the South African stockbreeder are here unknown, and the severest drought but slightly deteriorates the nutritious qualities of the herbage.

The soil of the large plains varies very little in any of the explored parts of the vast territory, and in such situations the herbage is very suitable for sheep, which here attain a size and weight far in excess of the Colonial average. The plains are, however, intersected by vast tracts of sand dunes resting on a white limestone formation, which probably covers a supply of water that, if tapped, would at once render the country habitable. These dunes are composed of heavy red sand, immovable by the winds, covered luxuriantly with nutritious grasses and shrubs, and here and there decked with a few large trees. They resemble huge Atlantic waves in form ; the hollows between them, being often two or three hundred yards wide, would afford space for sheltered homesteads, perhaps eminently picturesque, but certainly admirably suited for Boer occupation. Really copious rains fall in the Kalliharri at intervals of about three years, and when this occurs the whole country is covered with a crop of succulent watermelons, upon which live stock thrives exceedingly, and is quite independent of the absence of drinking-water. Showers no doubt fall every season in various parts of the desert, and the game, consisting chiefly of giraffe, eland, brindled gnu, gemsbuck, ostriches, and hartebeeste, swarm to those localities, safe from pursuit—as unless the melon harvest is general, and extends to the edges of the desert, no one dares · penetrate it beyond the distance to which water can be carried to sustain life.

These melons are called by the natives " tsamma," and are about the size of a round Dutch cheese. The flavour is insipid, and the water which the traveller obtains from them by cutting them up and simmering them in a pot over a slow fire is rather flat, but sweet and wholesome. The whole of this desert is singularly healthy for man and beast, except that portion on the north-east side immediately abutting on Lake N'Ghaami and the Botletle River. Even horse-sickness, although not unknown, is not very destructive in the Kalliharri, except in the districts I have mentioned above, and these parts are quite unfitted for settlement by white people. Strange to say, as yet no organised attempt has been made to explore the central parts of the " Thirst Land," which is only known to have been occasionally (in tsamma seasons) traversed by native hunting parties in search of ostrich feathers, and as a general rule few white men have done more than make flying excursions from the fringe of scanty waters on its south-west side, extending some thirty miles or so into its recesses. Nor does it appear likely that this region will be thoroughly explored until Government or some public body takes the matter up and goes to the expense of a properly equipped expedition for the purpose. Personally, I have travelled completely round the Kalliharri, starting from Uppington, on the Orange River, to Oliphant's Kloof, on the Lake, and back to the Transvaal viâ Khama's country. During the trip, which lasted over a year, by taking advantage of information derived from the wild bushmen of the desert, as to patches of available tsamma and an occasional pool of rainwater, I was enabled to penetrate these mysterious solitudes occasionally to some thirty miles or so distant from my stationary camp near permanent water—but in the absence of the necessary implements I was, of course, unable to explore for water, and certainly found none on the surface.

The pasturage, especially among sand dunes, was everywhere simply splendid, and grand sport with gemsbuck, eland, and ostrich rewarded well the risk and toil encountered. Giraffe were seen, but we did not hunt them, as at that time the waggons were heavily laden with meat and goods, with which it was necessary to hurry on to camp as fast as possible to avoid waste. During the current year (1894) an exploring expedition, under the auspices, I believe, of Mr. Rhodes, and conducted by a Dutch Church minister, made a faint attempt to penetrate the desert, principally with a view to ascertain the capabilities of the country bordered by the Botletle River for immigration purposes. As I have said before, that part of the country is, and must remain, unsuitable for colonisation on account of the prevalence of fever and of the most virulent thorn jungles to be met with in South Africa. It is said that on this occasion two faint attempts to tap underground waters were made without success, and the expedition was a failure—as I fully expected it would be under the circumstances.

In fact, no expedition of the kind should be undertaken in a perfunctory manner, and when on the edge of the desert some weeks should be expended in acquiring all the information possible from natives and other residents. No reliable information is, as a rule, obtainable in Africa in a hurry, or, in the absence of the last, it is necessary to " pump " without seeming to do so, or exciting suspicion. As a rule, the autocratic bearing of the ordinary cleric is a very undesirable quality in an explorer; the easy, luxurious lives of South African ecclesiastics are but poor preparations for travel off the high roads.

In ancient days the Kalliharri must have been about the best watered part of South Africa, with at least two deep broad rivers flowing slowly through the west part of it, and hundreds of smaller streams, in the beds of which the rounded stones prove that the water must have flowed for

centuries.   In some parts of the courses of the Oop
and Nossop Rivers the banks of the channels look
as perfect as if the waters had only left them a few
years ago, and the water marks on the rocky side
indicate that a depth of one hundred and fifty feet
was attained in places, with few fluctuations.   These
rivers were evidently navigable for hundreds of
miles without a break, and an examination of their
beds ought to reveal some interesting secrets at
least, in the absence of more tangible clues.   In
these river-beds all the usual indications of
diamondiferous deposits are plentifully strewed
on the surface at all events, and it is possible that
an explorer with the means of sufficient water at
hand to allow an efficient search might reap a rich
harvest.

In some few spots along the courses of the river
mentioned water has been obtained by digging
very shallow wells; while in other parts a well or
two dug by natives during a rainy season failed to
supply water at about eighty feet. Frequently
the natives will dig several pits pretty close to
each other, some of which will furnish clear fresh
water, while that in others will be brackish or even
too salt for the use of cattle.

In the interests of the Cape Colony nothing can be plainer than that a thorough experiment of the practicability of obtaining water in this fertile Thirst Land should be speedily made, as it is well known that the old Colonial pastures are over-stocked, and that the herbage generally is deteriorating in quality, as well as in sufficiency. As the country must eventually rely on wool and other pastoral products for revenue, the capture of additional pasture lands of first-rate quality, and nearly as large as France in extent, is a matter of paramount importance, more especially as those lands lie close to the Colonial boundary, and are approachable without danger to health or losses from tsetse-fly, or indeed any hindrance to easy locomotion and transport.

For my own part, I am under the impression that the sand-dune district should first be tested for water, which there would probably be found plentifully by boring through the limestone floor, which, though hard, is evidently not very thick. It is a curious fact that in these sand-dune districts the grasses are always green at the bottom, even when owing to droughts those on the hard plains are quite parched, thus presumably indicating approximate underground flow of the precious element so necessary to all kinds of life.

My first visit to this great Thirst Land occurred early in the fifties, shortly after the discovery of Lake N'Ghaami by Livingstone and Oswell. On this occasion I was accompanied by a valetudinarian whose acquaintance I made during a visit to Cape Town, and who had been sent out by his doctors to recuperate his very delicate lungs. I have reasons for withholding his name, although he joined the majority at a very good old age some few years since. He was a pleasant, clever fellow, but eccentric and obstinate to a degree typical of John Bull in excelsis. In those days no railway facilitated progress towards the far interior, and we jòlted patiently along in our bullock waggons over the thinly settled old Colony, enjoying occasional sport, till we reached a large native kraal called Kange, a little to the south of Mangwatto, where Seiomi, the father of the well-known Khama, then reigned. My plan was to stick to the hunting-road viâ Mangwatto, then reach the lower part of the Botletle, where it loses itself in reedy swamps of immense extent, and where elephants abounded. This road, which is still in use, crosses a corner of the desert, and the sand is very heavy, but water is found independently of rain at two places—Klobala and Tlacani—which, however, are about one hundred and twenty miles apart, and this distance must be covered without a chance of obtaining a drop of water for the labouring draught oxen, whose sufferings from thirst are intensified by the necessity of keeping them going night and day over this stretch of desert. This struggle involves great labour for man and beast, to say nothing of the anxiety and want of sleep for the four days and nights consumed on the waterless road. As a matter of fact, oxen seldom die of thirst if properly driven, on this route, and having reached the Tlacani Spring, the Botletle is then only thirty miles off, and all troubles with regard to water are over for the traveller bound for the Lake, as the track thence simply skirts the banks of the full river for the whole distance, except at spots where curves are avoided to shorten the distance. After striking the Botletle, at a kraal called Pompey, it takes about sixteen days, without stoppages, to reach Lake N'Ghaami, and even now there is no dearth of giraffe and smaller game, although the vast buffalo herd have deserted the river since a numerous Boer "trek" passed through the country some fourteen years ago and wantonly shot some thousands of them merely to glut the love of slaughter so characteristic of the race.

Most of the big game of South Africa stick to the localities where they have been bred till exterminated. The buffalo is the exception, and if he is much disturbed and cut up by mountain hunters he migrates at once, to be seen in his place no more, unless perhaps that locality is deserted for years by his human enemies.

However, to return to Kange: here I found that my friend D—— determined to take a bee-line across the desert for the Lake—which was supposed to be distant about twenty days—whereas by the usual track forty or more days would be consumed on the road. I found it quite useless to point out that there could be no water in the desert, or other hunters would have taken the short cut as a matter of course. D—— felt certain of finding water and reaching the Botletle without much difficulty. After a day or two arguing pros and cons we decided to part company, and D—— started, accompanied by an Irish servant named

Luck and three native " boys." Fortunately his waggon was, although roomy, very light—it having been built to my order and design in the Cape— and fourteen oxen in fine condition took it easily through the heaviest sand. D—— also took one horse, and a shower or two having lately fallen, he started in great spirits, and we agreed to meet on the Botletle at a kraal called Sibitan, where, while waiting for me, he would have any amount of hunting, as he was now quite strong, thanks to the effects of the desert air.

For my part, being a poor man, I did not feel justified in risking the loss of my nags, two waggon horses, draught cattle, and outfit, and so jogged along on the well-marked hunting track, eventually reaching the Botletle without loss, but not without a severe struggle, occasioned by the distances between the waters and heavy sand. All along the course of the river towards Sibitan elephants were very numerous, and as no other hunters had yet come up, they were unusually easy of approach —although the jungle was in places extremely difficult for a horseman to get through.

Having at length reached the rendezvous, and en route loaded my waggons with ivory, I waited a month for D——, but hearing nothing of him, at length turned towards the Colony, sadly satisfied that D—— had perished in the desert he so madly tempted. Meanwhile I reached Port Elizabeth in due time, sold my ivory, and fitted out again for the interior, meaning to hunt along the Limpopo and its tributaries. Having passed Sechele's kraal, while outspanned at a spring called Manhock, just eighteen months since parting with D——, all at once a waggon, with a very ragged white man leading the oxen, and an old Hottentot driving, came up. Going to see who it was, to my utter astonishment I found that the forlorn white man was my friend D——, very hungry, naked, tired, but in robust health. As I was well supplied, D—— was soon clothed, fed, and in his right mind, and we spent three joyous days together, during which he gave me the history of his strange adventures in the desert, and his final escape.

It appeared that after parting with me at Kange he got along on his course famously for some days, having found a few rainpools, which, however, soon dried up, and then suffering and danger loomed ahead. Of course he had loaded up a good supply of water for the use of himself and his people for some days, but as he would not listen to Luck, who wished to turn back, a mutiny broke out, and Luck and the "boys" determined to kill D——, take his properties, inclusive of £200 in hard cash, and endeavour to get back to Kange. Fortunately, however, one of the "boys" could not make up his mind to carry out the murderous plan, and gave D—— such detailed information that he decided if Luck's actions corresponded with those arranged to be acted on, that he, D——, would shoot Luck. About midnight D—— saw him creeping stealthily, gun in hand, towards his sleeping quarters. Then D——, who had taken a shot gun to bed with him, hesitated no longer, and Luck was killed on the spot. The "boys," with the exception of the one to whom D—— no doubt owed his life, at once fled, taking with them the horse, and as nothing more was ever heard of them, most likely they perished of thirst in the desert. By this time the oxen were outrageously thirsty, and when D—— and the "boy" tried to yoke them, they broke away and disappeared. No chance of saving life was now left, except the very faint one of leaving the waggon with such supplies as could be carried and tramping all through the sand on the course indicated by compass as leading to the Botletle. Therefore, taking with them a gun and some ammunition, some water in a large can, some dried meat and biscuits, with three bottles of champagne, which D—— had saved to drink with me when we should meet on the Botletle, the forlorn wanderers forged ahead painfully for forty-eight hours, when, just as all hope was lost, they crossed a thickly trodden game path along which a rhinoceros had lately passed. As the rhino is dependent on a daily supply of water for life, the travellers now knew that at least they would be saved from the awful fate of dying from thirst, and, stepping along with renewed energy, in a couple of hours a large deep and glittering pool of water was reached, and death was, for the time, cheated. Here elephants, rhinos, and other game evidently came to quench thirst, so that no danger of hunger was to be dreaded at all events, although poor D—— was about the worst shot with ball I ever saw, and ammunition was, of course, scarce until they could revisit the waggon and bring back the supplies. After quenching his intense thirst, and bathing,

D—— said he felt very hungry, as all the food brought from the waggon was consumed. No game, except a few hartebeestes and brindled gnus, was in sight, and after two fruitless shots they also took to flight.

Finding a huge and hideous puff adder, D—— killed it, cut off its head, and quickly grilled it on the ashes of a fire the Hottentot had made in the little thorny " skerm " which was to be their sleeping quarters. D—— and the " boy " supped royally on the beastly reptile ; found it very much to resemble eel, but hardly comparable to the club dinners in London, the thought of which, D—— says, were a constant source of annoyance to him during his long sojourn in the desert. With the advent of night, elephants, rhinos, lions, and other game crowded the margin of the pool, and seemed to care very little for the huge fire which D—— kept blazing, and eventually a huge rhino came so close to the " skerm " that D—— thought it incumbent to fire at him. The rhino bolted off a few yards and fell dead ; but it at length became necessary to scare the huge pachyderms by barking like dogs by turns, and thus by alarming the brutes gain a little exemption from the chance of being trampled upon, and a modicum of sleep.

Night after night these troubles were repeated, but gradually the skerm became impregnable to anything but an elephantine attack, and the game took to using the opposite side of the pool. The second day after arriving at this pool was wholly occupied by butchering the rhino and hanging up the meat to dry in the arid atmosphere, during which process a few wild bushmen arrived and made themselves useful. Fortunately the Hottentot could partially understand the bushmen's gibberish, and they were hired, for meat payment, to accompany D—— and his " boy " to the waggon to bring up supplies.

By a short cut the waggon was reached by one day's long march (say thirty miles), and everything was found untouched. With the help of the bushmen a good supply of things was brought into camp at the pool, but as the bushmen now knew all about the deserted waggon, D——, as a precaution against predatory instincts, previous to leaving it, had arranged a large heavily loaded pistol so that it would explode and hit any one climbing over the box-seat. This saved the cargo, as when D—— again visited the waggon the remains of a bushman were found in front of the waggon and the pistol had exploded. This unaccountable occurrence, indeed, so scared the thieves that they fled in dismay, and the cargo was saved.

For months D—— and his "boy" lived on monotonously, with fair comfort in a way, but at length some strange bushmen paid them a visit, and reported that early in the hunting season a white man from Walfish Bay intended trying to reach this water bent on elephant shooting. These people also told D—— that he had done well to remain stationary, as, in consequence of the failure of the melon (tsamma) crop, it would have been impossible for him to have reached the Botletle. D—— therefore very wisely decided to remain and wait the arrival of the elephant hunter, who in due time arrived, and turned out to be Mr. Anderson, a Swedish traveller and hunter of renown.

Here D—— and Anderson remained for some time together, and with the help of oxen the long-deserted waggon was brought into camp. Then rain at last fell, and a crop of tsamma soon rendered travelling possible, D—— bought two oxen from Anderson, and at last got out of the desert, if not without trouble, at least safely; and we met accidentally as I have mentioned.

Anderson was a first-rate elephant hunter, and I believe made a good bag at this pool, which has ever since been marked on the map as Anderson's Vlei.

The last of my visits to the Kalliharri was in 1879, and although the absence of tsamma circumscribed the extent of my wanderings from the beaten track viâ Twaart Modder, Kabeum, and Abekus Pits, I still found plenty of the superb gemsbuck and eland antelopes, and as these can be easily ridden into with a fairly good nag, they afford first-class sport. The gemsbuck is about the size and weight of a large donkey, and his action at a gallop is essentially asinine, although he gets along at a good pace and has no end of "stay." The straight horns are often fifty-two inches or more long, and, sharp as a rapier, are splendid trophies comparatively rarely included among the spolia of the African hunter, as the habitat of this animal is confined almost exclusively in South Africa to the desert, although now and then one may be found in or near Matabililand. Formerly I have hunted them on the south of the

Orange River, in the Kenhardt district, where they were very numerous, but are now probably extinct.

When driven to bay gemsbuck are apt to become dangerous and to use their horns with effect. On one occasion the horse of a Boer comrade of mine was transfixed and killed on the spot by a charge, the rider only escaping being pinned to the saddle by the position of his leg between the horns. These antelopes seem very indifferent to the attacks of dogs, as I once saw one which was pursued by a host of large native curs fight his way through, leaving five of his assailants dead or wounded behind him after an encounter which lasted only a few minutes. Natives assert that the lion is very averse to attacking the gemsbuck, and only assails him when no other game is available, very often coming to grief in the contest—which is, however, usually fatal to both combatants, if reports are trustworthy. The skin of this antelope is in parts more than an inch thick, and very much valued, being worth at least £2 in barter.

A rifle or gun to be good for gemsbuck should therefore have strong penetrating power, especially as most of the shots will be fired from behind although not necessarily from a great distance.

I mention this because I once saw a hunter empty the magazine of his ·38 Winchester (model 1873) in vain on one of these animals, which I had to put out of its misery with a ball from my 16 smooth-bore while it was still struggling along at a canter with some six bullets in it.

The ostriches of the Kalliharri are not only numerous, but furnish the finest feathers in the market, most of which are procured by Bastaard and native hunters, who ride them down and knock the whole troop of birds over with sticks, choosing a hot day for the hunt, as the birds are then more or less deficient in staying power.

Very fast horses are not required to run ostriches to a standstill, as the hunters never attempt closing with the birds till having rattled them along at a good pace the horses begin to get blown, when a halt is made, saddles removed, and the nags refresh themselves with a roll in the ·sand, their masters meanwhile enjoying a pipe. The birds, of course, very often disappear, but are also by this time glad to pull up not very far away, and this rest is fatal to them, as in cooling down they get stiff. When the hunters put on the next spurt the horses are soon among them, and the sticks busily applied to their necks with fatal effect. On these occasions no birds are spared, whatever may be the state of their plumage, as it seems that when run to a standstill ostriches pine away and die from the effects of over-exertion.

Some years ago the best white feathers were worth between £50 and £60 per lb., and the others in proportion. Some hundreds of natives were employed by storekeepers to hunt every season, and many closely packed waggon-loads of this costly product of the desert annually arrived at the Cape, but since ostrich farming has become an industry the price of feathers has declined at least by 80 per cent., and the hunt no longer pays expenses, although wild feathers still sell for more than those of tame birds.

Few white men have joined in this sport, as they are generally too heavy for their mounts, but as the natives of this part of the world are usually very light weights and capital horsemen, they had it all to themselves, and could have made lots of money had they not indulged recklessly in all kinds of extravagance as soon as they drew their pay. One Englishman of the historic name of Tom Jones, however, went into the desert boldly, and at the risk of his life reached localities where ostriches luxuriated in some natron-covered " pans " in vast numbers, and by shooting from cover he managed to get feathers which he sold for, I believe, £3,000 during his hunt, although only equipped with an old waggon, draught oxen, and an old Snider rifle. His adventures were marvellous, as were his escapes from death and thirst; but the wild bushmen gave him able assistance, and supplied him with various watery bulbs, which they dug in sufficient numbers to keep him and some of his oxen alive, and he at last emerged safely with his spoils, which he sold well. Eventually he invested the proceeds of his hunt in breeding cattle, and settling down at a spring on the outskirts of the desert, his herd increased so rapidly that when I last saw him he was a rich man in the prime of life, but quite determined to forego ostrich hunting for the future. He was a shrewd, uneducated man, who had travelled a good deal in South Africa, and had made a little fortune by diamond digging, of which fortune he was robbed. He gave it as his opinion that the Kalliharri country was the only part of the country where really successful stock ranching could be carried on, with, of course, the proviso that sufficient water can be raised. Brackish water is very healthy for man when once used to it, but its beneficial effects on cattle are very evident and indisputable, and probably the majority of waters tapped in this part of the country by the artesian or any other process would turn out more or less " brak," and in most cases admirably suitable for cattle, the market for which, as before stated, is chronically under-supplied throughout South Africa to such an extent that not only is beef a luxury, but condensed milk, Irish and Dutch butter and cheese, have to be largely imported for the supply of the mere handful of inhabitants peopling the immense areas within Colonial boundaries.

Blame for this state of things is undeservedly thrown on the Boers and farmers, but it would be more just to take rational account of the natural sterility of the country generally, the prevalence of diseases, and the results thus entailed on stock-breeding. By a successful opening up of the possible waters of the Kalliharri, and its occupation by settlers, the Cape would be far more enriched than by the discovery of any likely amount of gold—which naturally merely passes through the channels of commerce with Europe and returns no more to Colonial coffers.

Doubtless the success of the Transvaal goldfield has largely benefited the Colonies as regards credit and speculative profit, but it is an open secret that the interest of the aggregate capital employed to produce the gold output amounts to much less than the same amount of capital would produce, without any of the numerous mining risks, if invested in Consols. In the nature of things too numerous and abstruse to be here treated, it must be confessed that largely increased amounts of produce from the surface of the settled parts of South Africa can hardly be reasonably hoped for, whatever may be the value of the mineral resources of the country, and that in the interests of the future, when mining may—as is usually the case in the long run—be a fading and bygone industry, some strenuous effort should be made to open up new pasture lands within measurable distance of the old Colonial boundaries.

CHAPTER VII.

NATAL.

OF all the South African Colonies, Natal is the most essentially English, and as a residence for people with small independent means in search of a beautiful climate, fine scenery, and quiet but cheerful surroundings it would be hard to beat in any part of the world. A certain buoyancy of life seems to prevail in Natal strangely in contrast with the austere, puritanical surroundings which are so depressingly conspicuous in most parts of the old Colony; in fact, a good laugh and a cheering glass may be enjoyed in Natal without reproach, and the local Mrs. Grundy, albeit quite as estimable, is less positively conspicuous and oppressive than amidst other social coteries of South Africa. Young people flit about here in the fairly good spirits which it would be nearly criminal to exhibit in the west part of the Cape

Colony, or even among the "serious" populations in and around the more Anglicised East Province.

Living, as I have done for the past three years, in a village in the Western Province of the old Colony, I can safely say that outside my own little household I have never heard a pleasant rippling laugh; and I suspect any attempt in such decried art would impose not only a painful physical strain on the rigid facial muscles of the ordinary Africander but probably subject him to the censure of the Church, which he may possibly love, but most certainly abjectly fears. Cricket, football, races, and athletics are enjoyed in Natal; in the old Colony they are simply and gravely performed—not without skill, but entirely destitute of zest. Irrespective of mere years, Natalians are mostly young; Cape Colonists are generally aged. Such, at least, were my impressions formed during a residence of some duration in Natal some years ago, but I hear that gloomy moral clouds so strikingly at variance with the bright physical atmosphere of South Africa now to a great extent overshadow the town populations, and that the envy, hatred, and malice so characteristic of the "unco guid" communities are gradually ousting the spirit of " bonhomie " formerly characteristic of the little community of this little Colony. Be that as it may, the picturesque beauty of the country and the fertility of the limited areas of soil available for cultivation are unaltered. Fringing the principal lines of traffic, well-built, trim, and cheerful-looking homesteads rejoice the eye of the traveller from the more sterile districts of the greater part of South Africa.

The fruit and flowers of temperate and tropic climates abound in suitable localities, and nowhere perhaps within the small extent of a country—hardly so large as Scotland—can such varieties of climate be found and enjoyed, being, as it is, essentially healthy throughout. The great Drakensberg mountain range dominates the whole Colony, except on the Zululand border, and its spurs and rocky undulations are the chief components of this settlement. Everywhere pure water abounds, but although large streams, such as the Tugela, Umgeni, and Moie Rivers, flow through the land, they are not, and never can be, made navigable.

On the coast-line between Durban and the Tugela the sugar industries flourish to some extent in the rich alluvial plains, and tea is grown with an amount of success which bids fair to enrich the Colony substantially.

The higher parts of the country between Pietermaritzburg (the capital) and the boundaries of the Orange Free State and the Transvaal are, as stockbreeding areas, about on a par with the Cape Colony. In many localities the sheep do fairly well, but the runs are not very extensive. Cattle, if not of too heavy a breed, also do well in these parts, and although "horse-sickness" is sometimes prevalent, it is not so destructively fatal as in the Transvaal, and, indeed, its visits are fitful—with intervals of a year or two between them. Cereal crops grow well enough, but large spaces suitable for the plough are rare, and on most farms only amount to a few acres. Maize and millet are largely cultivated by the farmers and the numerous natives, as such crops do well in situations unsuitable for other cereals, and on them the Zulus thrive, and have generally a surplus for sale.

The Zulus, although living almost exclusively on "mealies" (maize), supplemented with a little milk, are a splendid race physically, and, although not of remarkable stature, are almost universally

strong, active, well-built fellows, as sleek as moles.
Satisfied as they are with their simple mode of
life, they feel too well off to care to work steadily
for any greater length of time than that required
to earn enough to buy some specified coveted
article. Unlike many other South African races,
they appear naturally averse to imitating the
white man in the matter of clothes, and are therefore but sorry customers to the "slop" seller when
living in their kraals; the law compels them to
wear at least a pair of trousers when in the towns
or villages, and here and there a Zulu in a
"go-to-meeting" suit is to be seen, but seems
hardly to enjoy the costume.

Missionaries are not successful among the
Zulus, who seem deficient in religious emotion-
alism, as contrasted with the mixed coloured races
who are town-dwellers; but an unregenerate Zulu
is generally honest and truthful, which can hardly
be said to be characteristic of the native convert
as a rule. Zulus are much employed as domestic
servants in Natal, and, as they are very cleanly,
honest, and fond of children, they do well in that
capacity, but as their women are not allowed to
hire themselves out, the office of nurse has often

to be conferred on a stalwart semi-nude male, who, however, treats his young charges with solicitous kindness and skill.

Durban, Natal's port, is the prettiest town in South Africa, situated as it is on its lakelike bay and surrounded by gentle elevations covered with rich foliage, from amongst which charming villas peep out of the Beria and elsewhere. The bay unfortunately is rather shallow, and its entrance is impeded by a bar which has seldom more than fifteen feet of water on it, so that large vessels cannot come in. Smaller craft, with the assistance of an able tug service, accomplish a passage easily and without danger, and discharge or load at a quay about a mile or so from the town, whence there is a railway.

Although the climate here is warm and apparently relaxing, the mortality is very low, comparing favourably with that of most English and Colonial towns. The streets and roads being now metalled, the sandy soil no longer impedes locomotion as in earlier times.

The public buildings and churches are substantial and handsome, and are, I think, built with a view to future exigencies rather than to the absolute requirements of the present. Pietermaritzburg, fifty miles inland, the capital of the Colony, is also a nice town, laid out with Dutch symmetry, and nearly surrounded by high and picturesque mountains. The climate is cooler than that of the seaport, owing to the altitude, and tropical fruits and produce are no longer seen growing, but the slopes of the mountains and hills are dotted with the pretty red-tiled cottages of small farmers, who seem prosperous, and at all events live in plenty and comfort.

The hotels in the towns and along the main roads are replete with all reasonable requirements, and no traveller need now fear having occasion to "rough" it more than in Europe.

Having ascended the mountain above Maritz-burg (by rail), a very cool atmosphere immediately makes itself felt before the little hamlet at Moir River, nestling in a warm and fertile hollow, is reached. Ascending again, the road to Ladysmith passes through rather a rugged country, where small Zulu kraals abound; here the first Boer immigrants fought many successive battles with Dingaan, and had to suffer also from a dreadful massacre, which cost six hundred or more lives, at the place where the village of Weepen (Weeping) now stands and rejoices in a quietude which approaches the oppressive. A little further on, and the spot where some five hundred Boers achieved their final victory over Dingaan is passed. Here, on my first visit to Natal, the bones of at least three thousand Zulu warriors covered the ground and attested the severity of the final struggle. Only a few Boers fell (I think eleven) on this occasion. The Zulus were unable to penetrate the Boer entrenchment of waggons and thorn bushes, although they renewed their assaults without ceasing for hours, and were swept away by the smooth-bore guns of the Boers, loaded with buckshot, till their bodies formed an extra rampart of defence.

Thence to the village on the fine Tugela River is not far, and crossing it, the traveller soon reaches Ladysmith, having covered one hundred miles since leaving Maritzburg, over a rugged upland country mostly suitable to pastoral pursuits on a limited scale. The parts of the country mentioned were not long since very difficult to travel over with waggons, and the fords over the rivers mentioned were often impassable for weeks at a time even by the ferries (ponts), and always more or less dangerous. Now bridges cross all these rapid streams, and the traveller rejoices on his way oblivious of the labours and perils of his pioneer predecessors.

Ladysmith is a nice neat village on the Klip River, but without much alluvial soil for gardens or much room for expansion. Many flourishing homesteads beautify the neighbourhood, but as a rule rocks and stone-covered hills prevail, and the towering Drakensberg range is always in sight on the way to the Orange Free State, and, at about seventy miles from Ladysmith, has to be crossed just beyond the village of Newcastle to reach the boundary of the Transvaal. On the road to the Orange Free State the range is also crossed, and the descent on the other side reveals the Boer village of Harrysmith, which is about the coldest inhabited spot in South Africa, as it is so over-shadowed by mountains that it enjoys only a few hours of sunshine every day, when the sun is visible only through the thick mountain mists.

Upon the whole, the modern fortune-hunter should avoid Natal, where he would find himself out of place ; but it is a nice little colony for small capitalists of moderate views seeking where the climate is good, living cheap, and native labour, especially of the domestic kind, plentiful. It is, however, a colony wholly unsuitable to the dumping-down of the ordinary emigrant dependent on wages, as on the coast coolies from India abound, and do all the heavy labour at a cheap rate, and the large Zulu population abundantly supplies other departments of the labour market. Clerks and shopmen are not in demand, and must not try their luck in Natal, as the ranks are full.

Sport in Natal is not very good as a rule, but in some parts heavy bags of francolin may be made with the help of a good pointer. Bushbucks are to be found in most of the rocky ravines, and leopards are not extinct in the same localities, but are difficult to get at unless beaters are employed. A few bustards, both large and small, are to be had here and there, as are also duiker and steinbucks, and now and again a reitbuck. Wildfowl are found wherever suitable pools exist, but such places are not numerous. A good stout 12 smoothbore C.F. gun, which will shoot ball well with one of the barrels, is all that is required in Natal, as although in the Ladysmith and Newcastle districts a few herds of protected hartebeestes roam about, it is difficult to get permission to shoot one, and a rifle is therefore a useless encumbrance unless for target practice. In the Zulu country, not far from the Natal boundary, hippos and alligators are fairly plentiful, in places, and even a few rhinos, buffaloes, and lions are still to be had in the eastern bush of Zululand near the coast, as are also elands, koodoos, brindled gnus, and smaller antelopes— such as reitbucks, impalas, and rosebucks. The country there away is feverish during the greater part of the year; all hunting must be done on foot, as the tsetse-fly abounds. The Natal country is unpleasant to ride over on account of the excessive prevalence of holes, stones, and impracticable "dongas" or nullahs. Everywhere snakes, too, are more plentiful than agreeable, and are both large and very venomous. Two species of mambas, one of the most deadly of the serpent tribe, ranging from six to eight or more feet in length, are often met with, and puff-adders, mountain adders, and yellow cobras are in places very numerous. Pythons are to be found near the coast, averaging from twelve to fifteen feet in length, but very thick in proportion. They are fairly numerous, and I must say that in two years spent in this Colony I saw more snakes than during the whole of my long sojourn in other parts of Africa.

The population of Natal may be taken at about 35,000 whites and perhaps 400,000 Zulus, but I do not anticipate any serious native outbreak in the future, as the intercolonial natives are contented and happy, and even if inclined for an outbreak, are so scattered in small kraals that combination would be impossible before efficient means for defence could be organised. The country throughout owes a great debt of gratitude to the late Sir Bartle Frere for breaking up the military organisation of the Zulu régime, although the cost entailed was great in consequence of the grievous shortcomings of Lord Chelmsford, which entailed the wholesale massacre of our 24th Regiment at Inshandwana, not to mention that of the Natalian Colonists who fell with them. The fact is, military officers are, as a rule, quite unfit for command in warfare with brave savage tribes, as has been proved by too many sad reverses in South Africa. The severe training for spectacular purposes prevalent in all regular armies, to the neglect of teaching the men the use of their weapons and habituating them to cultivate the hunter's instincts, militates against successful operations till some horrible mistake has to be repaired at a cost which need never have been incurred.

In the Zulu War the general in command seemed to ignore the fact that the enemy was essentially a brave one, as swift in its operations as good irregular cavalry, and as cunning as jackals. As a matter of course, ultimate victory could only be achieved at a great and unnecessary expense. These remarks may be taken for what they are worth, but anyhow our ultimate victory at Ulundi saved the lives of the Natal Colonists and the Transvaal from the effects of an invasion which would have been destructive at least of great numbers of isolated and defenceless people, although probably with very small loss to the Boer commanders, who would have made very short work of the Zulu hordes. Peaceful as things now are in and around Natal, it would be a great mistake for the Colonists to neglect training every man of capable physique in the efficient use of his horse and rifle, with the least possible amount

of useless military pageantry. An elementary
knowledge of a few simple movements is all that
is required for actual warfare, but the ability to
shoot steadily and accurately is of paramount
importance, supplemented as it ought to be with
practice in taking every advantage of cover and
acquiring a good rough idea of unmeasured
distances. Artillery is hardly worth the cost and
trouble of transport in African warfare, but
machine-guns are very valuable weapons, with
which all fighting bodies of men, whether troops
or civilians, ought to be adequately supplied.
Natal is now enjoying responsible government
and its cost. However, as the country is not very
extensive, and the natives pay a very appreciable
amount of taxes, administrative expenses ought
to be, relatively to those of the other extensive
and thinly populated Colonies, much less burden-
some, and let us hope the spouting community
in the House will be able to enjoy its pastime
economically.

CHAPTER VIII.

As a field wherein to give vent to the special aspirations of the globe-trotting sportsman, this little Republic holds out few attractions. Its vast bare and shelterless prairies are denuded of the countless herds of game life by which they were formerly tenanted, and the whole territory is now dotted with the rather widely detached homesteads of stock farmers, the majority of whom are, of course, Boers, although not a few of them are of English descent. A few villages, mostly inhabited by general storekeepers, represent the urban element. Bloemfontein, the seat of Government, is a thriving little place, and is adorned with public buildings of dimensions seemingly exuberant for its requirements, but very creditable, nevertheless, to the aspirations of such a Liliputian Republic.

K

The place is reputed to be unusually healthy, and a considerable number of consumptive sufferers use it as a roadside resting-place on their way to more permanent quarters. The whole place, however, is enveloped in a dense ecclesiastical atmosphere, which eclipses the brilliant sunshine of the natural article, and is hardly exhilarating to visitors not in urgent search of vicarious ghostly assistance. English "very-High-Church" officials in queer hats and sacerdotal garb appear spasmodically alert, and their immaculate philacteries flutter on the breeze in all directions, and are no doubt effective instruments of edification to the worshippers of clerical millinery. Fragile-looking nuns, seemingly in sadly depressed spirits, glide about the streets, and are, I believe, quartered in a neighbouring nunnery, which, however, was not built when I was last in this little metropolis. Monks there may be too, for aught I know to the contrary, as they are undistinguishable to the profane eye from the present High Church priesthood. Anyhow I can strongly recommend the place as splendid hunting quarters for aspirants to the honours and emoluments of monkhood, or appearances are more than usually deceptive.

The general condition of the inhabitants of the Orange Free State appears prosperous; although, perhaps, fortunes are not accumulated, wellbeing and content is a general characteristic of social life. The absence of wood for fuel in most parts of the country does not enhance the comforts of either the traveller or inhabitant, especially as for many months of the year a keen air prevails during the day and the nights are decidedly cold. For cooking purposes dung is but a poor substitute for wood, and the scent of it in a calcined state impregnates the food and atmosphere to an extent only to be ignored by long-acquired habit.

The Free State has been fortunate on the whole in the selection of its Presidents, and to young republics nothing is more essential than the competence of the head of the State, as his real position is autocratic. His Parliament is helpless as an initiating factor in politics, attributive to the prevalent narrow-mindedness incidental to the very limited education encouraged, or I may say hitherto permitted, by the omnipotent Dutch clergy. Signs are not wanting that the cleric will, in this respect, soon have to simulate a change of views, however disinclined he may be in reality.

Diamonds have been discovered and mined with success in this Republic, but it does not appear that any very marked results affecting the general welfare have as yet occurred in consequence. Indeed, the palmy days of diamond mining and dealing are visibly on the wane. The market for these indestructible gems has evidently been glutted by the Kimberley output, and although great skill has been employed to minimise the natural, and eventually inevitable, effects of an oversupply of such purely ornamental material, prices have ominously declined of late, and stocks in hand have accumulated to such an extent as to threaten the necessity of selling at any price at short date, or submitting to a ruinous retention of dormant stock for an indefinite period. Unfortunately, diamonds do not wear out, and are rarely lost, and the consequences of a glut of mere ornamental gems are not difficult to foresee, although likely to be lamentable enough to the holders of stock, either in the shape of scrip or stones, at no very distant date. In fact, the prosperity of the diamond industry depends on the maintenance of a very fragile artificial combination of contingencies, not easily controllable even by a Rhodes, who is certainly a man of incomparable business capacity in more ways than one, and who is, I have no doubt, perfectly aware of the fact that the existing diamond mines, if worked at anything like high pressure, would swamp any market reasonably to be reckoned on during the next century. As a matter of fact, the output of diamonds by the hundredweight is merely restricted by the interests of a monopoly.

The outlook for the roving sportsman in the Orange Free State is no longer a very tempting one, although here and there a fair day's shooting may be had. Springbucks are still visible in places, bustards of four varieties are not very scarce, and steinbuck, duiker, and rhebuck are far from extinct. With a good dog a fair bag of francolin may often be made, and in suitable places wildfowl are plentiful enough. I hear there are a few gnus and blesbucks still, but strictly preserved in a few localities.

Agricultural pursuits are but faintly in favour here, as the nature of the country and climate is not as a rule suitable for these occupations on a profitable scale. Here and there arable ground is worked, and a fair crop (mostly oats) is to be seen now and then. Maize, too, is to some extent grown, but the crops are not strikingly luxuriant in general. The Kaffirs also grow a little millet, but the needful supplies of these cereals are mostly imported from Basutoland.

The staple industry is therefore that of the grazier, and considerable quantities of wool and angora hair are exported. Upon the whole, as a stockbreeding country, the Free State is second to none, and superior to most of the pasture fields of South Africa. Horses, too, are successfully reared here, as the fatal African distemper, rightly termed " horse-sickness," if not unknown, is at least rarely destructive, and as its annual ravages in the Transvaal cause a considerable demand for remounts, a thriving business in horseflesh is a considerable element of profit to breeders.

CHAPTER IX.

HOW THE DIAMOND FIELDS WERE ACQUIRED BY
ENGLAND.

CONTEMPORANEOUSLY with the progress of the trial of the Claimant for the illegal means he had employed in the endeavour to substantiate a false claim to the Tichborne estates, a land swindle of infinitely more importance, if gauged by its political bearing and consequences, or by the value of the interests involved, was being carried on with success in a remote corner of South Africa. It attracted very little public attention at the time, and has since been relegated to oblivion by a profuse application of " hush-money," which Government found it expedient to provide in order to evade an exposure which represented national disgrace, and by the obliterating effects due to the lapse of time, combined with the extreme excitement caused by the development of the diamond mines. These mines absorbed the attention of the South African public for some years, during which the swindle was a working factor for the benefit of its originators.

At the period alluded to a Gladstonian Administration ruled the political roost, and Lord Kimberley was at the head of the Colonial Office. Mr. Gladstone was then a member of the "Little England" party, and therefore bitterly averse to Colonial extension as a principle; but the apparent value of the diamond fields proved an irresistible temptation to depart from the course of policy which was then in the ascendant. Annexation was decided on finally, the excuse offered being that by Imperial occupation only could the confusion locally prevalent owing to the weakness and incompetency of the Orange Free State Government, which was in possession, by purchase, of the richest diamondiferous area in Griqualand West, be reduced to order.

The real motive probably was that by a cheap acquisition of this glittering prize the Administration hoped to obtain an accession of popularity and votes.

The difficulties of the assumed situation were

very considerable, and involved the consideration
of the claims of the Orange Free State as well
as those of a multitude of settlers occupying
property within the diamondiferous, area. Clearly
the position taken up by the Imperial Government
was one of usurpation, and the only way to convert
it into that of legal occupation was by the purchase
of existing rights, or, failing that, by invalidating
them in some less honest way. Government was
apparently very averse to pay in coin for these
properties, and thus the position was becoming
rapidly untenable. At this crisis, however, an
adventurer, by name David Arnott, came to the
rescue ; for a consideration he offered to invalidate
the claims above mentioned, by a peculiar process,
provided he was allowed a free hand and no
questions were asked.

Upon these terms a bargain was struck, and the
fellow commenced his nefarious job. This Arnott
was a mulatto, reputed to be an illegitimate son
of a former Chief Justice in the Cape, named
Menzies, by a sable dam. Anyhow the Judge
behaved well in the matter, gave Arnott a good
education, and started him in life as a law agent
in the village of Colesberg, where his maternal

ancestress resided. To the considerable mental powers Arnott possessed others less admirable were added, and after a few years of practice in Colesberg, he found it advisable to remove to Griqualand West, where he became Secretary and adviser to Waterboer, one of the two reigning chiefs in that country. The name of the other was Cornelius Kok.

Arnott's scheme was to assert and endeavour to substantiate an "ex post facto" claim on the part of Waterboer to the position of having always been paramount chief, and that, as a natural consequence, all acts done by Cornelius Kok unauthorised by Waterboer's sign manual were invalid "pro facto."

This claim was an entire novelty—as fictitious as new—and if Lord Kimberley had taken the trouble to examine certain musty documents in his office, he would have become cognisant of facts proving the position of Kok as an independent chief, acknowledged as such formally by the British Government, and that Waterboer was never, in the native sense of the word, a chief at all, but inherited merely a "quasi" right to the position, as being the son and heir of his father, who was a headman appointed by the London Missionary Society to maintain order among the native converts in and around their station at Griquatown.

Kok's chief village was, and is, called Campbell's Dorp, and a deliminating line between his territory and that presided over by Waterboer was established. The existing dilemma was an awkward one, but Arnott solved it by forging some documents, by the destruction of others, and by falsification of the rest bearing evidence adverse to the claim of paramountcy. For reasons which, as Lord Dundreary says, "no fellow could understand" without implying a charge of their dishonesty against the Administration, Arnott's scheme was accepted and acted on. Officialdom on the fields was remodelled; two men—Bowker and Buskes—in prominent positions too honest to become "particeps criminis" in the swindle were dismissed.

The claims of the Free State and of the numerous British settlers who had acquired property under titles conferred by Cornelius Kok thus lapsed, in default of the signature of the fictitious paramount chief, and Arnott triumphed all along the line. In justice to Waterboer, it must be said that he resisted for a time and ridiculed the position imposed on him, but Arnott found means, by converting him from a decent, respectable man into a sodden idiotic inebriate, to obtain his assent to the fraud in the end, and he consented to become a Government pensioner to the tune of £1,000 per annum. Most of the British settlers were ruined and the Orange Free State ignored by the action taken by Government; but what of that? It obtained the diamond fields, and Arnott the hundred square miles of land (supposed to be diamondiferous) which was to be his reward for successful bravado. Within the above mentioned hundred square miles were many farms belonging to British subjects; most of them were persuaded by armed parties of natives under Arnott to quit, a small minority only holding out, and retained possession in spite of sanguinary threats. Not daring to resort to actual violence, Arnott determined merely to ruin these people by forcibly compelling some small Kaffir tribes in the neighbourhood to quit their own kraals and standing crops and encamp on the farms of the recalcitrant settlers with their flocks and herds, and then, by destroying the pasturage, annihilate the live stock belonging to the proprietors. This plan succeeded. Great numbers of cattle died of starvation, but the stubborn Britons, although much distressed, held on tenaciously till they were relieved, four years afterwards, by the results of the enquiry by the Royal Commission appointed by Mr. Disraeli, very shortly after his accession, and all the titles granted by Cornelius Kok were confirmed.

Meanwhile these men had lost four years mere profits, most of their live stock, and had to begin life again. One of them I know computed his losses incident on the Arnott swindle at £12,000.

As for the poor devils of Kaffirs employed as I have mentioned, their losses were even more severe than those of the white settlers they were compelled to ruin. Their standing crops were destroyed during their enforced absence from home by straying cattle, springbucks, and other causes; a great number of their live stock died; and such was the scarcity of food among them, that about three hundred of their number perished from exposure and starvation during the ensuing year.

All these enormities, with many others with

which I will not bore the reader, were perpetrated under the auspices of the Imperial Government, which for once in a way made a very judicious selection of its local representatives, in Griqualand West, for the purpose in hand. As a matter of fact, the appointees to office were, with few exceptions, men "under a cloud" more or less opaque. One Richard Southey, who had been a protégé and hanger-on of Sir Harry Smith when that gallant general was Governor of the Cape Colony, was appointed Administrator of Griqualand West. This man belonged to a family of farmers in the East Province, Cape Colony, noted for enterprise and bravery in Kaffir warfare, and was himself brimful of any amount of resolution and audacity. Government could count on him implicitly to carry out his instructions without any weak reference to morality, and he was therefore no doubt the right man in the right place during the Arnott régime. Fastidious people might not exactly admire his manners or his deficiency in education, but at all events he was a good servant to a bad Administration, and never, I believe, but once incurred censure, and that was for a trifling charge of £1,500 expended by him at an orgie " all among the Hottentots" at Griquatown. On this occasion this elderly Lothario capered about with his Hottentot Venuses, in full uniform as Her Majesty's representative, and no doubt had a good time of it, albeit rather a costly one to taxpayers.

Another official obtained a most responsible situation through the influence exerted to that end by a personage who shall be nameless here, on the ground that he had effectually aided in the escape of an alleged criminal of high degree, and, in fact, the whole lot, with perhaps one exception, were brilliant examples of the skill Government too seldom exhibits in the selection of its subordinate officers. At that time law in the diamond fields was only an obstacle to be trampled under foot at the caprice of the Administrator, justice a subject of ridicule, and order—of a kind—only enforced by the presence of troops occasionally requisitioned from the Cape when, by sheer tyranny, the diggers were at times driven to extremities. This state of things continued till, in consequence of the proceedings of the Royal Commission and the judgment pronounced by Judge Stockenstrom, a sudden end was put to it by the Cape High Commissioner, Sir Henry

Barkley, who, by virtue of orders from home, arrived at Kimberley in hot haste, and summarily dismissed the Administrator, and almost all the other officials—much to the joy of everybody else.

Shortly after this Major Lanyon was appointed Administrator, and if he was deficient in tact and talent, he was at least free from all tendency to turpitude. In view, however, of the national disgrace which disclosures made by the actors in the Arnott swindle might make public, it became imperative to provide against the probable danger by making satisfactory provision for those in possession of a dangerous knowledge of disgraceful secrets. Arnott was silenced by a pension of, I believe, £1,000 a year; Southey was not forgotten. Indeed, all the subordinate actors in this disgraceful affair were provided for at public expense, in some shape or other.

This was certainly a chivalrous act on the part of Mr. Disraeli's Government, if somewhat lacking in wisdom considered from an ethical point of view and in defiance of the sturdy maxim of "Fiat justitia, ruat cœlum." For my part, oblivious of possible political exigencies, I, after reading Judge Stockenstrom's summing-up speech, interviewed Major

Lanyon with a view to enquire whether criminal proceedings against Arnott were contemplated. His reply to my question was in the affirmative; he attributed delay simply to the non-arrival of necessary documents hourly expected. I can't explain this, but confine narration to facts. Personally, I was entirely disinterested in all Griqualand properties or affairs, but I shall never regret having been able to give information to the Commission which went far to expose this gigantic swindle.

As a natural consequence, the Orange Free State rights had to be acknowledged, and after some delay the Imperial Government purchased these for £90,000 down and a promise of an additional £15,000 at some future time to aid in railway construction. The cheap and nasty Gladstonian policy in Griqualand in the end turned out an extravagantly costly business. From first to last it is computed by competent judges to have cost in mere money a loss of about two millions, inclusive of nearly £500,000 for the Griqua war charges, about six hundred human lives, and the loss of all confidence in the honesty of the British Government. Hush money has been annually paid, at the expense of the taxpayers, for the last twenty-one years. I have no means of estimating the last-mentioned item with any precision, but these payments can hardly have amounted to less than £150,000 in addition. We are supposed to be governed by responsible Ministers, but perhaps this is only one of the prescriptive fictions John Bull so dearly loves—and pays for. It may be objected, with some show of plausibility, that the cost of the Griqua war should not be included as one chargeable to Gladstonian misdeeds, as the actual outbreak occurred during Major Lanyon's tenure of office as Administrator, but the fact remains that the real " casus belli " was the disaffection of the Griquas at having been " sold " by Arnott. The first shots fired were caused by the action of a magistrate appointed under the Arnott régime, in conjunction with two other persons whose acts of alleged injustice excited the natives into a state of frenzy. Two of these gentlemen are still living, but as I have eaten their salt I can do no less than decline mentioning names or giving publicity to the details of this lamentable episode. There is, I suppose, an unwritten statute of limitation absolving public men after the lapse of an undefined period from their responsibility for political misdeeds; in many cases it must be a fortunate thing for them. The memory of the electorate is notoriously very short, and the lapse of time affords ample opportunity for the concealment of evil deeds by very old-fashioned methods. Be that as it may, I have thought that an exposure of this great but little-known swindle may be of interest as marking distinctly the period at which the political degeneracy of Mr. Gladstone commenced

CHAPTER X.

THE TRANSVAAL.

HISTORICALLY considered, the Transvaal is the scene of disasters and disgrace to British prestige which will long be remembered, the ultimate effects of which have yet to be endured, and paid for, but cannot be recouped at a price reasonably approximate to the value of the material interests involved. It is difficult to pen a word on the subject of the craven action by Mr. Gladstone after the fight on Majuba Hill with any approach to patience or equanimity, and it is still more difficult to underestimate the crass stupidity and ignorance of facts exhibited in the instructions given to the officers who were, in the course of duty, compelled to conclude the humiliating Convention which terminated the Boer war.

The action taken by the Imperial Government in this case, fairly considered, admits of no excuse

or palliation—unless, indeed, abject panic can be pleaded as such; it was a flight from imaginary dangers very terrible to the eminently nervous constitution of the then Prime Minister, but at which a Lord Palmerston would have laughed.

Mr. Gladstone's rubbishy cant expression of his extreme desire to avoid blood-guiltiness at the expense of the Boers, and of his own magnanimity to an enemy by whom he had been ignominiously "sat upon," deceived none but those of his own "goody-goody" admirers, whose supreme pride is, it seems, to listen to and obey the eloquent and generally mysterious utterances of his unmatched capacity in casuistic dialectics. One of the "bêtes noirs" which precipitated the cowardly action of the Administration was a visionary idea that possible action in the only right direction would cause a rebellious rising of the Africander populations of the Cape Colony and the Free State. This was simply a "bogey" dressed up for a purpose. Even upon the assumption that racial tendencies might to a certain extent have influenced the sympathies of Africander relationship, the natural canniness of the race would in itself have been sufficient to confine hostile demonstration

within the limits of speech, or at the utmost of
negligible action. As a mere matter of fact, the
passive weight of the British Colonial population
was more than sufficient to neutralise any of the
possible antagonistic dangers arising from the
causes named, and every man of British origin or
relationship in South Africa would have risen in
support of just and patriotic action on the part of
the Imperial Government. But peace at any
price was the order of the day.

The Transvaal war was a warning as exemplifying the utter absurdity of the laborious and
disheartening system of the prescriptive military
training we so servilely copy from foreigners.
Our regiments—or at least those I then saw—were
composed of good-looking, serviceable young men,
faultless in " get-up," " military bearing," and so
forth ; good marchers, too, but, as it turned out,
utterly ignorant of the art of rifle-shooting, although
adepts at the " manual exercise." Both men and
officers were brave to an excess which astonished
the Boers, less in the way of admiration than as
indicative of a deficiency in common-sense.
Indeed, in every combat they stood their ground
till absolute slaughter, amounting once or twice

to more than 50 per cent. of their scanty numbers, compelled disaster. In the defence of the little isolated camps occupied our tiny garrisons were invincible, and it was in such places that they managed, at the expense of an incredible amount of ammunition, to inflict the greater part of the loss sustained by the Boers during the war— which amounted in all to about fifty men. In the battles fought in the open the Boers lost at Bronker's Spruit one man killed (a German named Keyser, whom I knew), and their losses at Lang's Neck, Ingogo, and Majuba could easily have been counted on the fingers of two hands— and leaving a digital balance to boot. Our losses by shot amounted in killed and wounded to something like 1,200 men, if the statistics I have seen, but have not now at hand, are correct. The Boer army consisted of perhaps 5,000 or 6,000 men scattered over a vast extent of country, and every man not disabled by age or sickness served in it. Of these numbers perhaps half were growing lads, and the rest of all ages up to sixty or upwards. Our troops were well armed with Martini rifles. The arms of the élite of the Boer army consisted chiefly of Westley Richards' breechloading carbines of an obsolete pattern, with paper cartridges. The remainder had a few breechloading rifles of various descriptions and bores, but muzzle-loaders of various sizes and sorts predominated until they were replaced by captured weapons.

Not a unit in the Boer army knew anything about "goose-steps," the "manual exercise," or military formations, but every one obeyed primary orders, and afterwards acted as his own general. The result was that, strange as it may seem, they actually out-manœuvred our officers on all occasions when tactics became a feature in the game, and their fire was most destructive. I have warred and hunted with Boers a good deal since making their acquaintance some fifty years ago, and observation of their shooting abilities impresses me with the idea that although there are fair numbers of very good shots among them, the average performance is not by any means so striking as that with which they are usually credited. Indeed, I can see no reason why any man with the necessary physique should not be able to attain to their average standard in this respect after, say, a fortnight's practice at varying objects at reasonable distances. Mere formal target-practice is in a general way merely a waste of ammunition, regarded as instruction for field work, and the absurd distances at which soldiers are compelled to expend the greater part of their far too scanty ammunition allowances a direct cause of deficiency in skill applicable to warfare. Inequalities in ground, woods, banks, hedges, and other obstacles will always compel real fighting to be restricted to within four hundred yards or thereabouts, allowing, of course, an occasional exception, rarely of much importance, in deciding the event of an action.

After our defeat at Majuba the victors were thoroughly ruined by the Fabian victories, their food was completely exhausted, their cattle and horses at Lang's Neck (chief camp) reduced to skeletons—which would have become carcases if they had been only exposed to one of the storms of wind, rain, or snow to which they would have been subjected by the advent of winter, which in that elevated region sets in early in April, one month after our causeless surrender on conditions. Ten pounds would have amply repaid Kaffirs for setting fire to the long dry grass on the line of the retreat, which weather alone would have compelled the Boers to attempt on the advent of winter; in fact, without firing another shot, they must have surrendered at discretion, or succeeded in finding shelter by capturing our strong fortified positions in Natal—which to them would have been certainly impregnable.

Our Government was either inexcusably ignorant of the nature of the country, the climate, and of the straits the enemy were reduced to, or wilfully ignored these things from unpatriotic motives.

Shortly after peace was concluded, I sojourned on a farm near the Oliphant's River for a few months; as the two sons of the Boer proprietor had fought at Majuba, conversation often turned on the recent campaign. I am bound to admit that the Majuba exploit was never spoken of in a boasting spirit by these young men, or, indeed, by any of the victors with whom I came in contact. From these conversations it was easy to gather the opinion that when the Boers began to attack the hill it was mainly with the intention of trying to discover the nature and numbers of the troops occupying the summit, and of taking pot shots at long range at any of the very conspicuous white helmets exposed. As the rocky nature of the ground was favourable to a safe advance, and as none of the English bullets hit anybody, the assailants crept on till within easy shooting distance, and then, being undismayed by the harmless showers of shot which passed yards over everybody's head, a rush for the top was made, and here at last one Boer fell. Then the English position was discovered to be mainly occupied by the dead and wounded who had succumbed to the accurate rifle fire of the Boers and a small disordered mass of men still on their legs, which soon dissolved under a deadly fire, took to precipitate flight, or surrendered as prisoners.

Such is a summary of a Boer account I heard of this miserable action; having conversed with many of those who participated in the victory, I come to the conclusion that the consensus of Boer opinion is that if our troops could only have used their rifles with moderate skill, the Majuba Hill could not have been stormed with success. The Boers, although individually brave, are traditionally averse seriously to contest a battle in which a heavy loss of life must be expended, and on occasions when such a result seems probable they, as a rule, very wisely retire and husband their scanty

numbers for a more propitious opportunity. I see
that in the opinion of those experts whose experience ought to count, the number of hits likely to
result from rifle fire in a general action is calculated
to amount to one-fifth of one per cent. of the
ammunition fired from the new magazine rifle. If
such is the case, or even if only a moderately
increased probability of improvement in the effects
of infantry fire may be assumed, it would really
seem advisable, considering the very scanty
numerical force of our army in proportion to the
work required of it, to take some effectual steps
to increase individual efficiency in the use of the
rifle, even if such a reform should infringe on the
excess of spectacular but somewhat frivolous and
vexatious occupations of our brave warriors.

As a matter of course, the retrocession of the
country inflicted a ruinous blow on those who had
put their faith in the permanency of Imperial
occupation, and invested capital on the strength of
their convictions, to say nothing of the losses incurred by individuals under the rank of capitalists,
who, actuated by the best motives, spent a good
deal of money in support of Government interests
during the war.

Personally, the war cost me about £400, and as, judged by an English standard, I am almost criminally impecunious, the blow was at least serious. Claims for compensation were indited it is true, and I put in one for about £300, which I previously submitted to the opinion of a Resident Magistrate, who pronounced it valid. Absence compelled me to act vicariously, and, not being " up to the ropes," I left no instructions for the application of palm oil—a lubricant very effective, I subsequently discovered—so I only netted a Government cheque for the magnificent sum of £27 10s. in full discharge of my claim. Multitudes of fictitious claims for large amounts, duly lubricated, passed easily, and were paid to people who afterwards freely boasted of their superior business knowledge and of its accruing benefits, not forgetting to inflict telling jokes at the expense of less astute people.

As a matter of fact, the slippery, dishonest, and cowardly conduct of the Gladstonian Government of the period demoralised almost everybody, and might be fairly pleaded as an excuse in mitigation of mere minor delinquencies.

During the first months of the Transvaal war

I suffered very little annoyance from the Boer authorities, and as it was conceded that I had done the country some service in former days, Vilgours, the Commandant of the Lechtenberg district, an old friend, allowed me to retain my battery of sporting weapons, besides giving me a protection from all requisitions of war. As a recipient of such favours I was then the only Englishman in the country. As a prisoner on parole I therefore quietly encamped on a vacated farm near Lechtenberg, where blesbuck and other game was plentiful, and passed a pleasant time awaiting the effects of the British triumph which I could not doubt as an approximate event.

However, a few weeks of this pleasant life having passed, Jan Vilgours was ordered to the front, and left this district. A rich, notorious miscreant named Greiffe being appointed in his stead, things got speedily unpleasant. Greiffe stole my horses, and threatened ominously when I complained, so I determined to break through the Boer outposts at any risk, and if possible reach the Kaffir territory of the Chief Monsioua. Of course I knew that if taken in the attempt I should be shot on the spot, but after consultation with my son, we decided to try and save, by decamping, the rest of our property, consisting of two waggons with their contents and twenty-four good draught oxen.

Having decided on this step, we spanned-in the waggons at once, and began our journey of fifty miles through a hostile country. Fearing to travel by the road, we bumped laboriously over rocks and other impediments till the first midnight arrived, when it became necessary to give the oxen a rest, and for that purpose drove into a thicket which completely concealed the bivouac. A good watch on a cross road one hundred yards in our front was kept in the bright moonlight, and soon, to our dismay, a patrol of three men was descried riding along slowly towards us. We hurriedly decided to shoot these fellows if we suspected they had discovered us, but seeing that they passed on towards the village, quite unconscious of our presence, we let them go in peace. As soon as possible we then spanned-in, and, after much fatigue and anxiety, approached the frontier line just at nightfall on the next day.

Here we met a patrol of two men, but as our force, inclusive of " boys," was superior, they were content to chat over matters in a friendly way, and after accepting a " soupie " of smoke passed on to their distant post. All was then plain sailing enough, although the remainder of the journey was performed in a tremendous thunderstorm, in the midst of which we reached a Kaffir outpost, where we met with hospitable welcome and recruited by a twelve-hours' rest before leaving for the Chief's kraal.

If any gentleman is curious to know the exact condition of his nerves, and has the opportunity of travelling through a hostile country at the rate of two miles an hour, with his little " all " stowed in two lumbering ox waggons likely enough to smash up at any moment, I strongly advise him not to neglect the opportunity, especially if he is in the act of breaking his parole.

At Mafeking we were received by Mr. Bethill and the Chief most kindly, and here we encamped till the news of the English defeat arrived.

To describe the rage and shame, caused by the surrender insisted on by Mr. Gladstone, throughout South Africa is beyond my powers. I am by no means an excitable man, but I must confess that on this occasion I could not help giving way to a paroxysm of rage and humiliation of which even now I do not feel at all ashamed.

The Transvaal mainly consists of an immense elevated plateau, shelterless, and exposed to terrific cold gales during the winter season, which oblige the stock farmers to migrate to the low bush country by which these vast prairie lands are encircled. Waving crops of coarse sour grass cover this elevated district, which are in a great measure burnt off during the winter in order that the stock returning from the bush veldt on the advent of spring may have the benefit of the young grass—then green and succulent. When ripe, this grass becomes unpalatable to stock of all kinds, and then, of course, condition rapidly deteriorates, and early in autumn very little milk is to be had, and but very few cattle are fit for butchers' use.

The pasturage in the low-lying encircling bush veldt is generaly of sweeter and better quality than that of the "high veldt," but in summer much of that country is scarcely healthy enough to attract permanent settlers, and insect pests so annoy live stock that they are not able to graze in the leisurely way essential to animal prosperity.

Agriculture in the Transvaal is only possible to

a limited extent, as arable land with water sufficient for necessary irrigation is only to be found in small patches, most of which are already worked assiduously by the owners, although perhaps not in the best possible manner. Every farm almost has a few acres under cultivation—limited by the amount of soil and water available, very rarely exceeding ten acres, but generally of less extent—possibly on a few farms one hundred acres may be under the plough, and I have once seen seventy-five acres of various crops on one farm in the Zeerust district. As farms generally consist of six thousand English acres, and often extend to twenty or thirty thousand, agriculture cannot be counted as a very prominent industry in a country the whole, or nearly the whole, of which is settled up to the mark of its competency to supply half of a white population of perhaps a little more or less than sixty thousand Boers of all ages and forty-five thousand Europeans, mostly adults, with the staple necessaries of life—the rest, together with all luxuries, being imported. It may be that some addition to the home-produced food supply might be obtained by the employment of adequate capital, more skilful methods, and increased industry, but at best the capabilities of the country from an agricultural and pastoral point of view are very limited and are handicapped by an unusual number of adverse contingencies. In the years which intervened between the cessation of British occupation and the opening up of the gold fields the sufferings of the people from poverty were very distressing to witness, although some of them had received considerable sums of money for land sold to English speculators during the occupation, and thus mitigated the severity of the situation. Had the discovery of these gold fields been delayed a little longer, actual starvation affecting almost everybody except the clergy and a few trading firms would have made fearful havoc among the poorer Boers, as the herds of game on which they had mainly depended for food and hides had disappeared, the victims of the most wasteful slaughter imaginable.

As a desirable field for agricultural operations the Transvaal is valueless, generally speaking, although individuals near the gold fields, and other favourable localities, are said to have made considerable moneys at times by a species of market gardening incapable of much extension. Stock-farming is simply a waste of time, money, and comfort, if the results of the business are calculated on the average profits of periods extending over, say, ten years, although at unfrequent intervals a slice of luck may turn up. Owing to the magnificent distances between villages and farms, the services of horses or mules are indispensable to all residents in this country, more especially to farmers. As the ravages of the fatal "horse-sickness" are annual causes of the loss of at least half of this description of stock throughout the whole territory, the item of deficit caused by this inevitable scourge seriously affects the prosperity of the country. About ninety-five per cent. of the animals attacked by this fell disease die, and the survivors, however defective in desirable qualities, being then considered acclimatised, become high-priced mokes of decreased spirits. Horses and mules exposed to the summer climate of the low bush veldt generally die off en masse during that and the autumn seasons. On high elevations the sickness is also fatal, but not to such a ruinous extent. Stabling seems to diminish the liability to disease to some extent, but in that case exposure to night air and dew, hardly to be avoided by the horses or mules of travellers, generally proves fatal. Indeed, in 1887, which was the last time I visited Pretoria, nearly every stabled horse in the town died, although at an altitude of, I believe, about 4,000 feet above the sea-level. How horse-owners have fared since I know not.

The rapid development of the gold fields at Johannesburg and elsewhere is one of the historical events of the age, and if the output continues to increase at the rate it has hitherto done, these gold mines will rank as the most productive in the world at no distant date. There is, indeed, little fear of any falling-off in the quantity of gold for an indefinite time, as the auriferous area still untouched is simply immense. Continued success is, however, mainly dependent on an uninterrupted supply of cheap Kaffir labour, in default of which most of the mines would have to "close down," and a case exemplifying the theory of the "survival of the fittest" would soon become the order of the day. Meanwhile there is little apparent cause for much fear on these grounds. These gold mines are entirely worked by companies, and as there is no alluvial deposit, they are wholly unsuitable for the working miner of any European race, who would certainly starve on the wages which satisfy the Kaffir.

Very few individual Kaffirs work more than a few weeks or months on the gold fields, which they come to with a view to obtain a certain fixed sum previously determined on, and having achieved their specific object, depart, and are replaced by fresh arrivals. Indeed, the majority of these black labourers are sent by their Chief to work for his, and their, own benefit conjointly, and on their return to the kraal a division of the acquired spoil ensues as a matter of course. House rent, taxes, and the other expenses of a white man on these fields are very serious amounts, only earnable by skilled artisans, of whom there is always rather more than an ample supply.

The administration of the government of this Republic is wholly in the hands of the President, Paul Kruger, and a clique of his favourite Hollanders. There is a Parliament, Council, or Raad, but, although not quite dumb, any recalcitrant member is very effectually silenced by the omnipotent Paul, who, on any symptom of opposition, rages in fierce texts from the Old Testament at the offender, who then incontinently trembles in his shoes in anticipation of wrath to come. Oftentimes these little scenes are varied by threats of Presidential resignation, and on such occasions apologies, regrets, and promises of amended behaviour for the future is the scene upon which the curtain is lowered, as the President picks up his stove-pipe hat, retires to enjoy a smoke, and, if in a liberal mood, indulges in a cup of coffee. His Honour Paul Kruger would in any other country than that in which he rules be looked upon as an extremely eccentric personality, repre‑ sentative of ideas long since obsolete, but manfully adhered to in defiance of the presence of modern "progress." His great popularity with that large majority of his constituents called "Doppers" is based on the profession and practice of a hard and fast puritanic régime, resembling that of Cromwellian times, upon the possession of a large amount of common-sense, a good reserve of "cunning," and undeniable personal courage. His literary acquirements are, or were till very lately, limited to a very intimate acquaintance with the sacred Hebraic records B.C. As a personification of extreme thrift he excels, and as far as mere utility is concerned £500 a year would supply him with every enjoyment just as well as the £8,000 he earns as President. But perhaps dissipation in the form of hoarding may be very pleasant pastime to the initiated, if they can only manage to ignore the extreme uncertainty of life, and the speed with which it passes on to the extreme limits only occasionally accorded.

In his younger days Paul was a "mighty hunter before the Lord," and flourished exceedingly on the profits made by the extensive tanning work he was skilled in. Game of all kinds abounded near his large estate in the Rustenberg district, and any quantity of hides was easily obtainable, as were also bark and other necessary articles. On this estate several hundred Kaffirs, under a headman named Kamian, were located and educated so far as to know that they were to perform all the varied duties of Gibeonites to the utmost endurable limits. These people were not ruled with rods of iron, and I never heard that whips of scorpions were employed to discipline them, but other instruments made of rhinoceros or hippo hide are very effective persuaders when wielded by muscular Boers, and the muscle and the whips were always to hand when requisite.

Gibeonites, and black ones at that, generally had to put up with a good allowance of " Sambok " treatment in those days, especially at the hands of the élite of the puritanical pietists, whose principles and practices were then in the ascendant. Kamian and his people at last got tired of this sort of thing; suddenly fled over the Marico, in a body, locating themselves very comfortably in a suitable place, where the tribe still lives in peace. Soon after this Kaffir exodus Paul began to take an active part in the curious politics of the country, and acted as Commander-in-Chief in several little wars, mostly with success. Shortly after the Transvaal war he was elected as President, and, in spite of his antiquated notions, the Republic has thriven wonderfully.

No deficiencies on the part of the Government could have arrested the prosperity of a country containing such successfully developed gold fields as those of Johannesburg, which began to attract efficient capital some three or four years after the signing of the Majuba Convention. Till that time poverty had reigned supreme, and unless the discovery of profital. gold mines had been timely made, the country would soon have been depopulated by emigration and starvation.

The country is eminently a black man's land, except as regards its mineral resources, as here the Kaffirs can in many situations, and without irrigation, raise the scanty crops of maize, millet, and . pumpkins upon which they contrive to live and thrive; and, living as they do under chiefs who administer their traditional semi-criminal laws, they are enabled to mitigate to a great extent the evils of indifferent pasturage by the frequent shifting of their flocks and herds, which seems, indeed, to be indispensable to the best attainable success in African stock-breeding operations.

Each white farmer in the country, of course, lives on his own property, and is thus debarred from the advantages the Kaffirs enjoy under their own social system, which suits them well, as they are by no means so addicted to litigation and quarrelling as their white Christian co-inhabitants. Of course Kaffirs indulge more or less in tribal warfare, which, however, is generally of a very bloodless character' (except when Zulus are concerned), and each man in his own tribe lives peacefully with his fellows. In spite of heathenism and polygamy, I have never witnessed in their

kraals any of those outbreaks of brutality or
indecency so prominently characteristic of large
sections of our civilised community. The Kaffir
population of the Transvaal greatly outnumbers
that of the whites, and upon the whole they now
enjoy good times, although in outlying districts,
such as Zoutpansberg, they are, or were a short
time ago, miserably fleeced by the officers employed
to collect the taxes.

The Government has persistently winked at
these practices, and allowed the local officers a
free hand. As a consequence, war broke out this
year (1894), which might have taxed the Boer
power very severely for years to come had the
Kaffirs taken united action. As it was, they mis-
managed matters, failed to support the common
cause by concerted action, and were defeated.
Had the paramount Chief, Magato, supported his
feudatories, as it was expected he would, the war
might have been prolonged for years, and, whether
victorious or not in the end, the Republic of the
Transvaal would have been by far the heavier
loser, as Magato's territory is singularly capable
of defence from its inaccessible nature to horsemen, or wheel transport, and so forth. If,

previously to the war with Malabock, to which I am now alluding, the Kaffirs had been able, or wise enough, to have made their case a subject of arbitration by disinterested judges, the Boer claim of sovereignty over the greater part of the Zoutpansberg district could not have been maintained. As it is, the Kaffirs have possibly forfeited, or at least very much enfeebled, their right to discuss the general question of ownership.

Upon the whole, looking the fact in the face that two-thirds of the revenue of the Transvaal is raised by the oppressive taxation of resident capitalists and others of the European races (chiefly British), who are refused political rights, and for many other reasons too numerous to go into here, the life of this Republic, on its present footing at least, is unlikely to be a prolonged one, especially if the extension and consolidation of European power and influence on the African continent is to emerge from the tentative, and assume a definite and permanent character.

It is simply absurd that a little community of the most narrow-minded and ignorant people on the face of the earth should be allowed to occupy a position giving them control over interests in the country worth at least ninety-five per cent. of those of the Boers—of powers of obstruction and annoyance in many directions, which, as shown by experience, they have a strong inclination to make use of on every possible occasion. Meanwhile, it is also high time that the meaning of the term suzerainty should be accurately defined—the duties and powers of the suzerain elucidated, in order that they may be carried efficiently into action when requisite for the protection of that important section of the Transvaal population now kept outside the pale within which the " Chosen People " monopolise the right of inflicting any amount of exorbitant taxation, and of exacting military service ad libitum, minus pay, food, medical attendance, or, indeed, any of the arrangements necessary to the welfare of troops in a campaign. This has been prominently evidenced lately by facts in connection with the late Malabock war, Her Majesty's High Commissioner at the Cape having had occasion to make a special journey to Pretoria to supplicate for the more indulgent treatment of British subjects by His Honour Paul Kruger and his myrmidons. Some sort of arrangement has been patched up in consequence, but it still remains optional with Paul Kruger to evade performance should caprice incline him to that line of action. We are in duty bound, I hear, to be thankful for the smallest mercies, and, if so, we ought to feel grateful that Uncle (Oom) Paul abstained on this occasion from "sitting on" our Queen's representative, which he would certainly have done had Mr. Gladstone been Prime Minister, if only to gratify the well-known taste for "long-suffering" characteristic of the G.O.M., and as some acknowledgment of the debt owing on the score of the "magnanimity" treatment of which he (Paul) was the imaginary recipient after his Majuba victory.

Paul is not a man to laugh much at any time, but he is said for once to have resisted the impulse to indulge in that weakness most boisterously, and that was when some one was kind enough to read to him Mr. Gladstone's exculpatory speech on the subject of the notorious Convention with the Boer Triumvirate of which Paul formed the prominent unit.

And now it may not be amiss to add a few lines embodying my opinions on the strained relations so long existing between the Transvaal oligarchy, the Imperial Government, and the Chartered Company, with the addition of an attempt to delineate the Boer character, and some of his habits, of which, for the most part, the authors of books on South Africa seem to me to entertain very elementary and superficial ideas, merely touching on such obvious facts and appearances as the most secretive, clannish people in the world expose to the view of Philistine travellers and sojourners within their gates.

It may be taken for granted that the British public is by this time quite sufficiently acquainted with the principles and details influencing the questions at issue between the Uitlanders and the Krugerian Government, and not a little wearied of being spectators of casuistic combats between Paul Kruger and Mr. Chamberlain, which combats are prolonged by the former merely with a view to gain time and concentrate any strength Kruger may acquire as the result of intrigues with any important European Power, or of those which are quietly but unremittingly employed to stir up hostile demonstrations among the rustic Africander population of the Cape Colony.

Surely the time has come when, if the Convention

of 1884 is to be maintained as the groundwork of British paramountcy in South Africa, it should be made apparent that the position is one of right, and not as that of a mere claim to be disputed, evaded, and frittered away by the Transvaal Government as being a concession on its part, enforced under protest, and therefore to be ignored at will whenever the opportunity for doing so may seem propitious. Until the position above alluded to has been defined specifically, and thus removed from the field of controversy, the elements of strife between the Imperial Government and the Transvaal will continue to smoulder, and unrest possibly, or rather probably, culminate in hostilities. But without prophesying, it is certain that if the Transvaal Government continues to play fast and loose with the Uitlanders' demand for an amelioration of their grievances, and to impose upon them the contemptible position of its mean Gibeonites to hew its wood and draw its water to order, so long will the peace of South Africa be dangerously jeopardised, and a minimum development of its resources, which are mainly mineral, will naturally result.

Taking all things into consideration, I think the

Uitlanders would, for the present at all events, do well to drop active agitation for the franchise, as even if it were granted it would be so surrounded by limitations as to be useless. Instead, insist, to the limits of peace, on just and fair recognition of the material grievances as affecting commercial interest, and on a total change in the attitude of the Transvaal Government as it affects adversely their just interests and possible prosperity.

To use a slang but expressive Yankeeism, the Transvaal President, who is practically an autocrat of a pronounced type, is actuated by a spirit of pure "cussedness" in all his dealings with any community outside the little class of those he fanatically believes to be the "Chosen People," and of whom he is the archpriest and prophet. The immunity from penalties, which he has so many times incurred, warrants him in supposing that the patience of the Imperial Government knows no limits. If its officials allow themselves to be deceived by specious words and promises, they incur the responsibility of the issue of dealings with a man who recognises no obligation to keep faith with Philistines. The spirit I have alluded to as the actuating factor of Kruger, and his clan,

is not one which can be referred to as expressive
of a mere exigency meant to confront an
emergency, but is an ingrained irreducible article
of faith which knows of no doubt or limitation.
The mischief which must one day, sooner or later,
result from persistence in such fanatical actions
must be prevented by the use of force in some
shape or other—moral if possible, physical if
necessary. Unless this principle is acted upon,
evil days, with civil war, and a struggle for
supremacy in South Africa are imminent.

That the Transvaal Government is prepared to
show its teeth, and use them too, if a favourable
occasion presents itself, is quite clearly proved by
the excessive amount of arms of every description
it has lately imported; and I use the term excessive
advisedly, I think, as not only is the Transvaal absolutely immune from the remotest danger of hostile
aggression from any quarter, but the armament it
possesses is sufficient for the equipment of four
times the number of burgher warriors it could put
into the field. In the absence of exact statistics
this may be approximately estimated at between
fifteen and eighteen thousand men between the ages
of sixteen and sixty—and of these at least one-

third would be physically unfit for anything but sedentary employment for defensive purposes.

This being so, it naturally follows that without being unduly suspicious it may be concluded that the Transvaal Government has, or thinks it has, arranged for outside support. The enigma as to the quarter from whence it is to be obtained, and as to the objective of hostile aggression on its part, remains unsolved, but is nevertheless worthy of the consideration of the Imperial Government. Possibly, when the question as to the amount of the indemnity to be paid to the Transvaal on account of the Jameson Raid comes under discussion, some light may be thrown on these questions, as the extravagantly insulting amount claimed can be considered only as a direct challenge intended to raise an issue, but by no means as an account likely to be seriously entertained with a view to payment. I may, of course, be mistaken, but surely all the evidence we have goes to prove that the main object of the Transvaal Government for the present is to gain time to formulate and organise with a view to future hostile action; and if so, it most certainly follows that the first duty of the Imperial Government is to insist on a prompt settlement of all matters in dispute on a practical and satisfactory basis. Failing which, an ultimatum is the only alternative—always supposing that all demands on the Transvaal are framed in a thoroughly just and even a conciliatory spirit.

However, I am not concerned to go into details as regards the present accumulating political troubles in South Africa. I trust that public opinion in England is becoming aware of the fact that all these complications may be traced to the effects of Mr. Gladstone's imbecile and sentimental policy, consequent on the result of our miserable little disaster at Majuba, and that safety for the future can be secured only by reverting to a course within the bounds of practical politics.

To attempt a description of the Transvaal, compressed within the limits which I have decided on, would be a vain endeavour, but it may suffice to say that in appearance at least it would compare favourably with any part of South Africa. A traveller passing over its upland in the summer season, looking over a boundless expanse of grass waving in the wind like a corn crop, would at once naturally conclude that, limited as its arable area is, at any rate it is surely a rich pastoral country.

He would fail to realise the fact that this herbage is coarse, sour, and unacceptable to domestic cattle except for the few weeks in the year when the young grass springs up on patches which have been burnt off during the winter. Then bleak weather, with violent gales, oblige the Boers to take, or send, their cattle into the sheltered belts of low bush veldt by which this immense plateau is surrounded at a lower level, and where the grass, if not very nutritious or plentiful, is at any rate not unacceptable to cattle.

Under these adverse circumstances the Transvaal Boer contrived to exist while the myriads of ruminating game, such as elands, blesbucks, and other antelopes blackened the plains and not only provided him with meat but with hides which he could readily barter away for the few groceries and clothes he required, without diminishing his scanty and gradually decreasing herd of cattle by killing or selling out of it. The squalor in the midst of which the generality of the Transvaal Boers were quite content to exist during what may be termed the " Game period " was something which can hardly be imagined by Europeans— even if perchance they have visited the very worst parts of the West of Ireland. There were, of course, exceptions to this rule, but they were few and far between, and in these individual instances consisted of men who had left the Cape Colony comparatively rich in flocks. Hundreds were eating up their capital in a country where to hope for any reasonable increase of live stock from mere breeding sources is a delusion. In spite of the frequent mention of "Our beloved country" and so forth in official documents, the Boers have really no attachment to it in the patriotic sense of the word, and since the final extermination of the game their only wish has been to "trek" to any available country now suitable to the successful pursuit of the only industry of which they are capable—that of stock farmers.

With a view to a wholesale exodus, they have been continually fitting out expeditions for the discovery of a promising country; all expeditions have been disastrous failures from one cause or another, but chiefly from the enmity of the fever-fiend and thirst. No doubt they would have anticipated Mr. Rhodes and occupied Matabeleland long ago could they have persuaded their leaders to organise an expedition strong enough to attempt an invasion, but as the leaders were mostly men in official positions, who were, as a rule, making their small piles by a systematic pillage of the Kaffir tribes within or near the Transvaal boundaries, an organised movement in sufficient strength became hopeless. Shortly after the restoration of the country by England, poverty and famine prevailed to an extent which will never be known to any but eyewitnesses, of whom I was one; and had the discovery of gold been delayed for a very few years, the Transvaal would have become a huge cemetery for the majority of its inhabitants. This may seem now to be an exaggerated view of the situation prevailing at the period alluded to, but it is nevertheless a substantially correct one. The providential discovery of gold alone averted a catastrophe in the very nick of time, just as Sir Bartle Frere's destruction of the Zulu power had previously saved the Transvaal from wholesale massacre, which, ruined and but poorly furnished with obsolete arms, and no ammunition to speak of, the Boers would have been powerless to escape from, or at best could only have saved their lives by flight and by sacrificing the whole of the live stock on which they were dependent for a living. The usual result of indebtedness thus incurred has intensified the enmity of the Boers towards their benefactors, and although they must know that every one of them is indebted in a greater or less degree to the industry, skill, and enterprise, to say nothing of capital of Englishmen, the only acknowledgment they have made has been signally displayed by an accentuated expression of contempt, hatred, and oppression for the very people to whom most of them are indebted for their lives, and all for the prosperity they now enjoy.

Notwithstanding the facts which prove the justice of the above allegations, these wretched and intensely ignorant people have conciliated the admiration of a considerable clique in England and on the Continent, by whom they are credited with all kinds of patriotic and domestic virtues. If a love of their country can be assumed from the fact that they have already sold almost every square mile of it, of any present or prospective value, to mining companies or speculators, they may claim the title awarded to them, but on no other grounds. Meanwhile, the much-abused Uitlander is the proprietor of more than half of the Trānsvaal area and of nineteen-twentieths of the entire assets of the territory which I have just managed to escape calling a republic.

Having previously adverted to the system of plunder of which the Kaffirs are the victims at the hands of the minor officials of the Government, I will mention one instance of it which is within my own knowledge, and which occurred just previously to leaving the Transvaal, some eight or nine years ago, and while I was on a visit to Zoutpansberg. In this case a party of some twenty Kaffirs were returning to their homes from the Randt gold fields, which were then just beginning to promise a rich harvest, and had nearly passed an official residence when they were halted to order and called upon to answer a charge of having washed in the water-furrow belonging to the official in question at a point some two miles or so distant from the homestead. They were at once summarily convicted without trial, and had to submit to having their packs opened, the confiscation of the cash found in them, and, if memory does not deceive me, the exact sum extracted was a few shillings in excess of £47. The Kaffirs were then allowed to proceed on their way, and to retain their blankets

and other trifles. But to go into details of the
isolated cases of sheer barbarity of which parties
of Kaffirs travelling home after a spell of work—
either on the sugar plantations of Natal or from
the gold fields—have been made the victims, would
be to write a series of "shockers" differing only
from those usually published under that title as
being narratives of fact as distinguished from
fiction. For many reasons I decline the task in
favour of the historian of the future, should such
an individual turn up.

It must be borne in mind, too, that any narrative
of mine would be strictly confined to circumstances
within my personal cognisance, and therefore in-
complete, and would relate to events of past times
occurring some time between 1870 and 1890. If
we may judge from current reports and occasional
newspaper paragraphs, the system has been per-
petuated—although possibly the more flagrant acts
of barbarity may have been eliminated as a rule.

In fact, the animus and actions of the Transvaal
Government are a disgrace to civilisation, and that
it is allowed to control the lives and fortunes of
the British and other Uitlanders upon whom it
preys is discreditable—to use a mild term—to the

Imperial Government. The sufferings are evidently irritating to the French Government at least, many of whose subjects are largely interested in the gold industry, the prosperity of which it is the policy of the Transvaal Government to minimise or destroy, with a view of depressing the share market till measures are ripe for bringing out the companies and converting the property so secured into a huge Government monopoly.

Indeed, in the existent state of things it is simply absurd to prate about British supremacy, paramountcy, conventions, and the rest, unless such pressure is applied as will compel the Transvaal oligarchy to abandon its Chinese attitude once for all and link hands with all concerned in developing the latent resources of South Africa. However inferior the country may be in what I will call surface value, it is more or less throughout a highly mineralised country but very slightly prospected. Whether such a disagreeable state of things can be consummated peaceably or otherwise remains to be revealed, but the sooner a crisis of some sort is brought about the better. Otherwise dangers and difficulties will continue to increase, and it can hardly be wise or creditable to defer finalities till we may possibly be involved in the great contest which seems to threaten the peace of Europe within measurable time.

It must not, however, be inferred from the tone I have adopted that I am in favour of heroic action. It is certain that if the Imperial Government fails to enunciate a definite policy embodying the principle of continuity as a basis, all assertion of paramountcy will amount to a farce very likely to terminate in a tragedy.

The perusal of many works on South Africa has led me to conclude that among the authors of those productions a very decided and favourable opinion of the religious and moral character of the Boers is usually expressed. For my own part, in the absence of any definite standard which authorises one to pronounce judgment on such very recondite matters, or to appraise the value of any man's religious belief, or practice, I feel incompetent to advance any decided opinion. I shall confine myself to a narrative of the impressions gathered from a close observation of overt facts during a residence among these peculiar people extending over at least a generation.

The real unsophisticated Boer is perhaps more

priestridden than it is easy for an ordinary Englishman to understand. When you know him intimately, and are careful to avoid controversial topics, it very soon becomes apparent that his religion is largely conventional, and so interwoven with superstition that an expert alone could assign it an adequately descriptive name, or appraise approximately its spiritual value. The priesthood, or ministers, among these people enjoy the advantage of being credited by their congregations with semi-supernatural endowments as being the accredited brokers or agents through whom alone all spiritual business can be effectually transacted, and are habitually spoken of as " Gezent van den Heires " (Heaven-sent Messengers), and it is therefore not surprising that these envoys accept the position with its accruing advantages, acquire a good deal of property, and enjoy to the fullest extent at least " otium " and locally at least a large allowance of the " dignitate." I use the word locally advisedly, as neither their manners nor culture would suffice as claims to a share of the latter distinctions amongst any other than the semi-civilised community they exploit. These reverend persons as a rule confine themselves to the performance of ritualistic duties, and ignore all intimacy with their disciples outside the church walls, or, if they do pay an occasional visit to some of the richest of them, that is the extent of their extra-mural labours. A poor Boer family need never fear being made the objects either of their charity or condescension.

The criminal statistics of the Transvaal may be ignored as any guide to the amount of existent offences against the law, but as a matter of justice I feel bound to say that crimes of violence or larceny are of rare occurrence among the Boers (always exclusive of their dealings with the natives), neither can they justly be accused of drunkenness or rowdyism.

On the other hand, it is a matter of notoriety that incest prevails amongst them to an extent happily unknown elsewhere. Such at least was the case when I was a Transvaaler. As substantiating this charge, I may mention that some of the last months I spent in the Transvaal were passed in the district of Middelburg; that within a radius of not more than ten miles from my camp three abnormally atrocious cases of the crime alluded to were notorious, and had been so for some years. The law was in none of them used as a deterrent agent; stranger still, the guilty parties forfeited no social standing as a consequence of their universally admitted guilt—although illicit connection with coloured females entails a sentence of the severest form of ostracism. So much for the prevalent habit of the almost universal customs of straining at gnats and swallowing camels as easily as oysters. Obviously I am compelled to omit mentioning the names of all these criminals, but am not precluded from indicating their personalities. Sad to say, perhaps the worst offender was a rich old Boer of pious proclivities, inasmuch as at his homestead church services were usually performed once a quarter, and that he was an elder of the congregation. Another of those to whom I allude was a field-cornet in Government service; and the third implicated was, I must admit, considered a loose character all round, and was only just tolerated by his neighbours, but the objection to his society was consequent on rowdyism, not on the guilt incurred by the commission of the crime I name. I have no reason to think that these practices were at all more prevalent in the district I have mentioned than in any other, and if I were inclined I could enumerate many cases quite as notorious and easily to be authenticated in various other parts of the country. The subject is, however, a distasteful one to dilate upon in detail; I should have avoided mentioning it had it not been necessary to elucidate the very peculiar features of the religious and moral life of the Boers—some of whom I have known to quote texts from the Old Testament exculpatory of those guilty of this sin.

The library of a Transvaaler is one of the compactest possible, and is often comprised in the possession of a huge brass-bound Family Bible. The most treasured is one full of engravings representing Biblical events and personalities, not to mention others whose habitat is said to be either in more blissful regions than we are at present acquainted with, or in the horrible depths of the infernal territories. The normal Boer firmly believes that these engravings are as correct in details as photographs. Sometimes, or perhaps generally, a few hymn-books swell the tale, and— that is all. The clergy discourage as much as possible the perusal of any other kind of literature ; the Boers have no desire to disobey their behests. These people, indeed, rarely read anything but Old Testament records, and profess to find in them all the spiritual nutriment they need, evidently considering the New Testament as a work of secondary importance, although they are by no means inclined to forego the title of Christians. Right or wrong, such is a sketch of the impressions in regard to Boer religion which have been forced upon me by observations, and I merely mention them for what they are worth, be it much, little, or nothing.

The insane rage for the acquisition of territory in Africa which prevailed a few years ago seems fortunately to be abating as the knowledge of the unfitness of the country generally for permanent occupation by European races increases, but even now the influx of immigrants in search of the rapid fortunes they so foolishly hope to make either at Johannesburg or in Rhodesia is threatening a catastrophe of serious import in the near future, as the Cape Colony, the Transvaal, the Orange River Free State, and Natal are being rapidly denuded of a sufficient supply of food for the existing sparse populations. If the rinderpest should, in the southern parts of the country, rage with the virulence it has done in the more northern districts, actual famine will certainly result. The territories I have mentioned are, even at their best, too sterile to support a sufficient supply of live stock adequately to supply present demand. It is fruitless to expect that the gaps already made in the cattle stock by rinderpest and increasing droughts can be filled up within the necessary time. Unpopular as my opinion may be, it is full time to confess that South Africa is, if we except its mineral productions, one of the poorest countries on earth, and that everywhere Nature opposes successfully all attempts at improvements on anything like an important scale.

People point in vain to the speed with which countries like Australia and Argentina recuperate after suffering severe losses of stock from drought, and argue that South Africa might do the same. They forget the fact that in the countries alluded to the herbage is all, or nearly all, acceptable to all kinds of live stock, which therefore rapidly increases; that in South Africa the exact reverse is the case, at least eighty per cent. of the grass and bush being distasteful, and in many districts even poisonous, to the live stock. These remarks do not apply to some of the Karroo districts, where the herbage, although very sparse, is fairly good for sheep.

At the present moment, although the revenue shows well, thousands of natives and hundreds of white people are dying of fever and famine in various directions, and but little notice is taken of these horrors—and the end is not yet. To an English reader this state of things seems paradoxical, but is explained by the fact that the Government coffers are filled by the rush of trade to the diamond and gold centres over Government lines of rail; by customs dues and the like on goods in transit. These goods are paid for in gold and gems, and the profits become the property of foreign or English shareholders and speculators; only the fraction of a small percentage remains in the country to benefit the Colonist, who, as a rule, lives in a hand-to-mouth fashion perforce.

If the country could pay for its imports in wool or other pastoral products, naturally all surplus profits would be enjoyed by the inhabitants of the land, but as these products are only worth between three and four millions per annum, comparative or actual poverty stares the South African colonist full in the face, and in the event of anything occurring to preclude the profitable working of the diamond and gold mines nothing could save the country from insolvency, seeing that its debt alone amounts to more than twenty-seven millions. The interest on this debt is mainly dependent for realisation on the output of minerals. If this or anything like it is true as regards the present and prospective situation, how then is it that Cape securities rule so high? We live in a gambling age, and no amount of financial temerity is surprising. Anyhow, intending emigrants to this country, or to Rhodesia, will do well to pause before they decide to embark, and to bear in mind that living in the golden city costs at least three times as much, and in Rhodesia ten times as much as in England; that the prices for provisions, and as a consequence of all necessaries, are rising rapidly, and such comforts as a well-to-do artisan in England is accustomed to are the monopolies of the millionaires.

A glance at the map of South Africa is sufficient to convince any one that eventually, and even very soon, Delagoa will become the port of entry for almost all imports destined for the Transvaal markets; Natal will probably retain a certain share in the business, especially if it is practicable to reduce harbour dues and other shipping charges and the railway tariff, but the Cape Colony will, I fear, be left out in the cold, and the revenue now derived from rail traffic will shrink to a vanishing point in as far as it may be affected by an almost total loss of all but intercolonial business.

I hope this may prove a pessimistic view of the prospects of the Cape in the near future, but fear it will turn out to be more correct than desirable to well-wishers for the prosperity of the Colony. Meanwhile we are living in a fool's paradise; our legislators seem much more inclined to authorise expenditure than to advocate economy.

CHAPTER XI.

RHODESIA.

My last visit to the vast regions now comprised under this name having taken place in 1879, I cannot pretend to enlighten the reader on subjects connected with the development of the country since it has become a British possession. The acquisition of Rhodesia reflects honour on all concerned in the operation from its conception to its completion; and whether looked at from a military or administrative standpoint, it is unique in the absence of that increment of blundering stupidity which has generally been so prominent a factor in the conduct of all South African affairs of a prominent character, in which a "native question" has been an integral component. Indeed, the whole business is not only creditable to the gallant men employed in the acquisition of the country and its retention in spite of the determined efforts of the warlike Matabele to eject them, but to the Home Government, which for once in a way was wise enough to ignore "red tape" and allow a free hand to competent men, with the result that the Chartered Company may fairly lay claim, as far as past action is concerned, to adopt "Sans peur et sans reproche" as its motto.

The financial success of the Chartered Company will, I think, depend entirely on the amount of profitable gold exhumed within its territories, as, although the capabilities for pastoral and agricultural operations of many parts of Matabeleland and Mashonaland are at least on an equality with those of any of the settled parts of South Africa, it is obvious that the success of the farming population must depend on a good local demand for produce. Mining centres will, if successful, ensure the prosperity of the farming community as a matter of course, and the cost of living on these mining centres will compare very favourably with such expenses on the Johannesburg gold fields, situated as they are in a part of the country where the commonest necessities of life have to be imported loaded with all the charges of lengthy transport. Other things being equal, the mining camps within the Company's territory will reap the benefit of a local supply of the necessaries of life equal to any demand likely to occur, and when the Beira Railway is completed machinery and other imported goods will in all probability be delivered at the townships or camps at moderate cost, and without the ruinous delays incidental to waggon transport.

To obtrude my personal impressions in the form of opinions on the special value of the auriferous areas within Rhodesia would be an act of inexcusable rashness, as when I travelled in these parts my objects were simply those of the ordinary nomadic sportsman, and I was then, as now, quite innocent of any practical knowledge bearing on mineralogical subjects. However, I was impressed as early as 1853 with a floating idea that the greater part of what is now the Chartered Company's territory was more or less auriferous, and, indeed, obtained from the natives several vulture quills full of " gim "—more or less rounded grains of gold, evidently the produce of what I believe Cornish miners call streaming. The specimens mentioned were obtained from Malakas wandering over the plains to the south-west of Matabeleland, and were probably the product of river beds to the north-east, where gold has been obtained by both washing and mining from pre-historic times, until the Zulu raids under Umziligazi gradually put an end to native industry in this direction.

The immense auriferous area within Rhodesian limits forbids the idea that the mines have been worked to exhaustion by native processes, and there must be an almost inexhaustible number of virgin reefs awaiting development in any case; and that such is the confident opinion of those who have already invested in properties of various sorts here is evidenced by an apparently lavish scale of expenditure on public building, etc., by the emigrants, although tangible gold results have not yet been handled, owing to the enormous difficulties of transport by ox-waggon viâ the Transvaal, the great extent of unhealthy country to be slowly plodded through before reaching the healthier heights of Matabeleland and Mashona-land, and the occurrence of the late war with Lo Benguela and his bloodthirsty ruffians. The Beira Railway, when complete to Salisbury, will

at once clear away all transport difficulties affecting the north-east parts of the country, which have
probably the richest gold-bearing possibilities,
with the advantage of agricultural facilities at
hand in a fairly healthy climate.

Reverting to golden prospects, it is quite on the
cards that the lately annexed Matabeleland may
become the chief mining centre of the country.
Practically this part of the country has never been
prospected for gold, owing to the strict prohibi-
tions of Umziligazi and his son Lo Benguela, who
visited with relentless vengeance any attempts to
obtain a practical knowledge of gold prospects
within his immediate territories. Even the superficial examinations of Matabeleland which date
from the very recent conquest of the country
disclose the undeniable fact that gold-bearing
quartz-reefs abound in all directions, and the only
question bearing on the future importance of the
country at present partially unsolved is simply
that of the percentage of the precious ore in its
matrix of quartz, as although Matabeleland proper,
in the absence of the high altitude of the Mashonaland plateau, can hardly be expected to possess
the great advantages of a bracing climate, it is

upon the whole healthy enough to be comfortably and safely inhabitable by the northern European races.

As a stockbreeding country Matabeleland is at least equal to the best settled parts of any portion of South Africa, and in that respect my impression is that it will be found superior to the more elevated country of Mashonaland. Upon the whole, the prospects of pastoral and agricultural settlers in any parts of Rhodesia likely to be permanently occupied by immigrants are decidedly cheery, conditional of course on the success of mining operations. In the absence of such success I must candidly confess that I do not think that any settlements in tropical Africa of national importance will achieve enough success to compensate adventurers for the numerous difficulties and drawbacks incidental to the general nature of these countries, where up to the present a conspicuous dearth of exportable commodities in adequate quantities is at all events the rule. Here and there, even in the absence of gold, the energy of modern progress will doubtless eventually dot over the whole of the healthier portions of the African continent with isolated trading posts, mostly dependent on the ivory trade, which, however, must be considered, from its very nature, to be rapidly advancing towards a vanishing point.

Should success become the eventuality of the efforts of the Chartered Company, the results will in all probability be more far-reaching and important, both financially and politically, with the advantage too of an unprecedented rapidity of consummation, than any yet recorded in Colonial annals.

As a base of action commanding the route through Africa to the Nile sources, with a view to the speedy substitution of legitimate commerce for the interior slave trade so long carried on with impunity by the Arabs and natives in their employ, Rhodesia is invaluable, connected as it soon will be with the Blantyre settlements on Nyassa by a chain of military posts, whence a junction with forces to be organised in Uganda will ensure the prosperity of the greater part of Central Africa in as far as peace can do so. The distances between the Chartered Company and the Nile sources are certainly "magnificent," but so also are the promised results, if indeed England really means to make a great national effort to introduce civilisation and commerce as a dominating power in the Dark Continent.

It is also obvious that nothing but brute force should compel us to evacuate Egypt, which in our absence would speedily become a mere raiding-ground of the Dervishes until again helped out of her troubles by the energetic action of France, which she would only be too glad to exert in reconquering the Soudan, and thus acquiring an indisputable and permanent claim to the occupation of Egypt.

The presence of a settled system of Government extending from the confines of Zambesian Rhodesia to the sources of the Nile is now easily within the region of possibility if the requisite energy is available; and the moral effect of action on the indicated lines would go far to weaken and demoralise the Dervish position on the Nile, and extinguish all hope of a rallying point in the rear of the North Soudan.

In a country like Rhodesia, next to the profit-able output of gold comes the question of certain and reasonably speedy means of transport and communication, and along what may be considered

the main arteries of communication which are to
supply the wants of the country as regards
travellers and merchandise for given centres of
business, provision is being made by the approaching completion of the railway from Beira and of
the projected continuation of the line from British
Bechuanaland, but the difficulty of maintaining
essential intercourse between the various scattered
villages and homesteads still remains to be provided for, not to mention the necessity of providing
the means of swift locomotion for the semi-
military police force which is an indispensable
requisite in such a country as Rhodesia.

Experience obliges me to assume that the
severity of the fatal " horse-sickness " which prevails in many parts of South Africa, and with more
intensity in tropical South-East Africa probably
than anywhere else, precludes the hope that the
country can ever be supplied with acclimatised
horses or mules at all nearly adequate to the
demand. The introduction of unacclimatised
animals means a death-rate at short date among
them of probably ninety per cent. at least, and
may be regarded as a fruitless and ruinous
expedient. It is true that in the Transvaal a

few acclimatised horses may here and there be picked up if expense is no object, and that perhaps one-half of the number of these animals may have survived an attack of the real "horse-sickness," which the Boers designate as "dikkop sikte," and many—perhaps indeed a majority of those animals—will be able to withstand the effects of the Rhodesian climate. The remaining half of the horses sold as "salted," or acclimatised, have perhaps survived an attack of the milder form of the disease, locally known as the "din sikte," and all or most of these will speedily die during their first experience of a Matabeleland summer, the result being that the price of a well-known acclimatised horse, without reference to quality, may be quoted at about four times his selling price as an "unsalted" animal. Indeed, the most miserable old moke, if really "salted," readily commands prices ranging from £50 to £75. Good hacks may be bought in any requisite number in the Cape Colony, Natal, or the Orange Free State for from £10 to £15—minus, of course, pedigree qualifications—as in these parts epidemic "horse-sickness" is of too unfrequent occurrence to affect prices.

Such being the case, it is evident that the time is fast approaching when it will become imperative for those interested in the country to look the question in the face, and, discarding prejudice, to consider whether it would not be wise and profitable to follow the example of the Queensland (Australia) colonists, who, under pressure of the same kind—resulting, however, from a different cause, imported camels, ten thousand of which are already doing satisfactory work in that Colony. I do not think, however, that the heavy transport camel chiefly in demand there would find favour here, but the light, swift camel which the Arabs use only for riding would be the ideal animal, not only for police mounts, carrying of posts, and keeping up communication throughout the north-west portions of British Bechuanaland and the Rhodesian territory generally, but as a means of rapid locomotion for individuals whose business requirements preclude the possibility of sedentary habits. Subject to experiment, there can be little doubt, moreover, that these animals would breed and thrive in any part of the country, and it is incontestable that upon the coarsest and scantiest food they will cover more ground in three consecutive days than any but an exceptionally good horse can in four, or even five, upon the best food. In all respects, in fact, they are, for the purposes of African travel, far more suitable than horses, even if horses could live in these parts of the country I am just now treating of. True, these beasts are not attractive in appearance, and are deficient in good manners, but they are eminently fitted by nature for African travel, and, in short, where horses will not live, are, I submit, indispensable to the safety and wellbeing of settlers in such countries as Rhodesia.

So much has been written on the subject of the game animals of the country that I will only remark that, although pretty well stocked in parts, sad and wasteful havoc has already reduced the numbers of the larger and more valuable of the fauna in the more accessible districts, and unless effective measures are speedily adopted to preserve the existing remnants, extermination will speedily be accomplished.

If, however, the £100 license to shoot the larger species of game animals which has been lately imposed by the Chartered Company is made strictly obligatory, under heavy penalties for in-

P

fraction or evasion, the destruction of the game animals will be averted, as hunting parties cannot traverse the African veldt without detection, at least by natives, who would be only too glad for a small remuneration to report the presence of such as might seek to enter the country by routes unprotected by police stations or the presence of permanent officials.

English hunting parties will not be deterred by the payment of £100 from gratifying their tastes, and it may be added that such parties, composed as they naturally are of men with true sporting instincts, as a rule avoid committing the unnecessary and cruel slaughter which Boer hunters delight in, and universally practise. These people, armed with long-range small-bore rifles, indeed, never can resist the temptation of pumping a stream of lead "into the brown" of any troops of game within sight, picking up only those animals which fall on or near the spot where they were hit, and taking no trouble whatever to try and secure any of the numerous wounded which are left to die miserably without compunction.

The almost universal use of small-bore rifles (inclusive of ·450-bores) has played the mischief with the game all over the country, without, I think, increasing the number of animals actually brought to "bag." The reason for this is that animals of a certain size (say up to three hundredweight) do not afford sufficient resistance to projectiles to cause an expansion of the bullet, and therefore make but a small external wound, in consequence of which little or no "blood spoor" is visible generally, to enable or encourage a man to follow up wounded game, which is thus left to perish from internal hemorrhage, but is lost to the hunter, as under such circumstances the extraordinary vitality of almost all African game animals, with the exception perhaps of elands, suffices to enable them, although mortally wounded, to escape actual capture.

Personally, and for the reasons mentioned, after sufficient trial I soon gave up the use of small-bore long-range rifles, and reverted to one gauge, 12-bores, specially made smooth-bores or rifles, or ·577-bores, for all kinds of game with satisfactory results. One of the mischiefs attending the use of small-bores is that, in spite of oneself, one is often tempted to fire a lot of risky and ineffectual shots at long range and without taking sufficient pains to obtain a fairly certain shot, thus disturbing the game over a vast extent of country to very little purpose. In fact, in the interests of real sport, it would be advisable, where a rule can be enforced, to prohibit the use of small-bore long-range rifles altogether, and to oblige all hunters and sportsmen applying for a license to confine themselves to weapons of not less than ·577.

I suggest this as the result of experience in the African hunting veldt extending over upwards of forty years, and although I am well aware that exceptional individuals I could name, and could count on my fingers, can and do make effectual and sportsmanlike use of the weapons I condemn, and restrict themselves to firing at distances up to which it is possible to calculate on hitting fatal spots. The £100 license will certainly be effective in prohibiting the ravages of Boer hunting parties, especially if such parties are not allowed to consist of more than two hunters each, besides their necessary attendants.

Lions are still plentiful enough in many parts of Rhodesia, although incomparably few in number as compared with those which used to frequent parts of the Orange Free State and the Transvaal in my earlier sporting days, where game then positively swarmed. However, the English globe-trotting sportsman bent on killing a lion or two need not fear disappointment, although the prevalence of high grass and pretty thick bush militate against making a large bag of such cunning and wary beasts.

No part of tropical South Africa, indeed, ever within my recollection exhibited such a show of all kinds of game as could be seen on the banks of the Limpopo and on the lower parts of its tributaries further south, where it was, during the fifties, impossible to look from any vantage point, such as an anthill, without seeing numbers of rhinos, giraffes, buffaloes, and smaller game among the thickets of low white thorns which are almost peculiar to the narrow alluvial valley through which the Limpopo winds its tortuous course. Elephants, too, often frequented the banks of the river, but were chiefly abundant on the higher levels of the country around, much of which was then infested by the tsetse fly, which disappeared as the big game became gradually exterminated.

The valley of the Limpopo and the neighbouring country abounds in the finest pasturage in South

Africa, if some parts of the Kalliharri be excepted, but the presence of an acute form of African fever precludes the hope that it will ever be settled by stock farmers, although some of them may make use of it during the healthier season—from May till about November.

At present Rhodesia, great as its ultimate possibilities may be, is not, I think, a country to which a poor man can be conscientiously advised to go unless under a contract providing work of a specified kind and for a certain term. Mere unskilled labour is sufficiently supplied by the natives at a very low rate of pay, and as time advances this source of labour supply will be always adequate to meet any possible demand for the rough work requisite in mining or agricultural pursuits. Englishmen have every reason to be proud of the success of the brave few who have added Rhodesia to the Empire, and every inducement to aid and assist the development of this promising territory is fairly within view of the speculative classes who have supplied the impetus to which such great success in South African enterprise is due.

*   *   *   *   *   *

Since writing the foregoing remarks on Rhodesia, another serious little war has involved Matabeleland and Mashonaland in a costly and cruel contest. Rinderpest has utterly destroyed all the cattle, and, great as may be the wealth and talent at the command of the Chartered Company, it is difficult to entertain any great hope of its ability to develop the country satisfactorily within any reasonable time, especially as permanent peace appears improbable; and, indeed, a very unsatisfactory contest is still raging in Mashonaland.

It suggests itself to my mind that if these territories are to be successfully colonised, the system of giving out farms to individuals for isolated occupation must be abandoned as unsuitable to the nature of the country and as dangerous to an unwarrantable degree. The prosperity of stock-farming in South Africa depends mainly on the ability to shift live stock from post to post as frequently as may be necessary or expedient. To keep stock in any paying quantity in any circumscribed area in South Africa is to cause the herbage, of which only a very limited percentage is of any value, to become stale, and thus invites disease and intensifies its effects. I would, therefore, with deference, suggest that it would be well for the Chartered Company to take this suggestion into consideration, and to select suitable village sites for the occupation of settlers, allotting, of course, a fair amount of arable land (Erven) to each homestead. Each such village should possess a right of common of as large an extent as possible or necessary, suitably provided with the necessary waters, to which localities stock, under the direction and control of the village Council, should be allotted in suitable lots and shifted from place to place as may be expedient. This is, in fact, the native system, and as regards success the main results are unquestionable, and the Kaffirs have as a rule raised two beasts for every one on detached private farms—equal numbers of breeding cattle being taken into consideration, and in spite of the fact that the Kaffir management of important details is very faulty.

Indeed, some such scheme is worthy of being seriously thought out and applied to further the best interests of Rhodesia, if the country is to be converted into a colony instead of being, as it now is, a mere area for disreputable bogus speculations and intrigue.

CHAPTER XII.

ON EMIGRATION TO SOUTH AFRICA.

MANY sources of really valuable statistical and general information on the subject of emigration to South Africa are now available to enquirers, but the points of view on which writers approach the question vary so much that it may not be superfluous to treat of it from a novel but perhaps somewhat eccentric standpoint, intended not only to be descriptive of things as they exist but explanatory of the causes of which they are the effects.

As the poorer class of emigrants are more in need of reliable information than others, it is but just and right to address them first, and seriously to point out the dangers and difficulties which are incurred by those who are destitute of helpful friends already settled in the country, or such as take a leap in the dark and have neglected to secure a situation previously to leaving an endurable existence at home. At present—that is to say, early in 1898—no fairly well employed artisan nor unskilled labourer should imagine he will achieve betterment by coming to South Africa, and the same advice applies even more forcibly to mercantile clerks and shop assistants.

In fact, the supply of labour in these industries very much exceeds any demand likely to arise within the near future.

Above all means let nothing tempt any intending emigrant of limited means to entertain the idea for a moment of bringing out a wife and family to any part of South Africa if he is not in the situation to place them in a home at once. Preliminary expenses during the time usually spent in search of a billet are ruinous, and generally previously to getting settled a stranger to the country will have to do a lot of costly travelling.

I may mention, too, that in commercial establishments employers generally make it a rule never to employ a married man when a bachelor is available. In the mining centres, in many of the towns, and here and there on farms, a limited and fluctuating demand for skilled labour exists, with wages varying with localities, and as a rule slightly in excess of the home rate. In exceptional cases the remuneration for that class of labour rules very high on paper, but then the enhanced expenses of living in localities where these excessive wages are paid is antagonistic to an improved balance to credit.

Shop assistants work generally about sixty-four to seventy hours in the week, but in most parts of the country and villages get a weekly half-holiday, and as a certain thing throughout the country a certain latitude as regards dress and bearing prevails, and men and women of this class are allowed to express themselves with the best language and with the best pronunciation their individual culture permits of—which would be an offence in England to certain high-class customers. However, the demand for this kind of work is very limited, as the Colonial-born youth of both sexes are filling up vacancies efficiently; and inasmuch as they not only speak Dutch but generally better English than is usually heard in the same class at home, they compete successfully, especially in country districts, with newly arrived emigrants. I think aspirants of the class alluded to would do well to take " Punch's " advice to aspirants to matrimony, which was—" Don't! "

It is observable that many of the numerous clerkly class who have lately poured into these Colonies are not physically fit for Colonial exigencies, and have come out upon the assumption that the climate is a specific in cases of pulmonary complaints. This idea is erroneous as regards the infinitely greater part of inhabitable South Africa, although true as to certain localities, where, as a rule, employment is unobtainable, the population doomed to be eternally sparse, and discomfort of all kinds endemic among the dreariest aspects of nature. For instance, on the bare, windy, and dust-coloured Karroo district, where life becomes a burden to all except to stolid Boer or native, and here and there a European who has lowered his standard of life to a state of chronic endurance mitigated by Cape smoke or Dop brandy. I have thought it a duty to offer these opinions on the prospects of the uncapitalised hordes of immigrants which have for some time been dumped down on South African soil, and are, in largely increasing numbers, in a pitiable condition of at best semi-starvation, with the near prospect of fatal results as their best hope, for there is no provision in these countries for actual pauperism, and with the exception of here and there a millionaire who has made his pile by speculations to which various descriptive epithets might be applied, the mass of the population is living from hand to mouth, though very generally hardly up to a standard worthy of being classed within the sphere of financial morality, but amply fulfilling the duties of that vulgarised ostentation which has become of late the dominating religion. This leaves no margin for the effective application of the funds necessary to mitigate the miseries of Colonial paupers, and so these poor creatures disappear in squads into as yet unexplored depths, and their fate is as little mentioned or noticed as possible, although no doubt shrewdly suspected.

Free hospitals for the sick poor are conspicuously absent in South Africa, and the sufferings of the impecunious invalid surpass in misery my powers of description, or any parallel adduced by comparison of what we hear of in the slums of great European cities.

Unskilled labour in these Colonies is delegated as a rule to the coloured population, and paid for by a pittance upon which few Europeans could sustain health, or even life, but which suffices to supply the less elaborate necessities of the coloured races.

It would be vain to attempt to name the average earnings of the coloured working classes, differing as they do to such extraordinary extents in divers localities. In and around the village in which this has been penned efficient agricultural labour commands from 10s. to £1 a month, and light work, such as driving and the care of stock, is performed by youngsters at various prices according to age and capacity. Near the seaports wages for rough labour and domestic service commands a price commensurate with the increased expenses of living, but by no means approaching the English standard if we take into consideration the relative prices and qualities of necessaries which in South Africa are very much dearer than in England.

Coloured people seem to be able to live and dress fairly well somehow, but herd together in groups and spaces which would be revolting, if not impossible, to any decent English workman, and would even be considered "hard lines" by the submerged residuum of the slum population.

Indeed, the prevalence of "dress" among the young coloured females in the towns is somewhat startling as contrasted with the wages they receive as domestic servants, but it is quite possible that experts "in the know" may be able to account for the discrepancy.

Up to the time of the discovery of diamonds, some thirty years since, the Cape Colony represented a vast Sleepy Hollow with two moderately well-to-do seaports, a few somnolent villages, and a rural white population composed chiefly of Boers and the minority of the descendants of the English settlers of 1821 inhabiting the best portion of the Eastern Provinces. Here and there, in the desolate and sterile Karroo and in its bordering mountain ranges of the Nieufeldt and Sneeberg, a few adventurers were settled as sheep-farmers, and were struggling manfully with the adverse nature, inherent in the African soil and climate everywhere as far as I know, with a measure of success just sufficient generally to keep their pots boiling, but poor enough as representing cash dividends on the capital invested. A restful state of stagnation prevailed, and millionaires, misery, and progress were unknown entities. Serious native wars had ceased, and the loss of the Imperial expenditure since the advent of responsible government was keenly felt, as the Colonists began to find out that a white elephant was a very expensive and dangerous acquisition to maintain.

In the sixties and in the beginning of the seventies the Colony was fast drifting into absolute insolvency.

Capital flowed quickly out of the country; immigration had entirely ceased; the profits derivable from agricultural and pastoral enterprise were insufficient to meet the demands of the Exchequer and other creditors; people began to see that in such a generally sterile country any material increase in these productions might be a matter of hope but not of expectancy. When financial matters were nearing their very worst, the richest diamond field was discovered in the Orange Free State, a few miles out of the Colonial boundary; emigrants flocked in, capital accumulated, the Imperial Government jumped the diamondiferous territory in the manner previously treated of in detail, Colonial bankruptcy was avoided, and progress initiated in its stead. Then extraordinary activity prevailed for some years at the great diamond camp, Kimberley, and gave an impetus to trade such as had never before been anticipated.

In the then absence of the omnipotent rail, the roads from the seaports were choked with waggons slowly dragging up supplies of all kinds, inclusive of all sorts and conditions of men, to the desolate semi-desert where the glittering gems teemed. Employment at remunerative rates abounded, and although disease and death in those early days claimed a heavy tribute, South Africa was jubilant at emerging from stagnation. But the diamond fields are no longer the hunting-grounds of the immigrant, as the mines are now owned and worked by the great De Beers Company, whose one aim is to limit production to within the demands of the world and thus keep up prices, and as long as this powerful company retains its monopoly diamonds will rule at high prices, but if by any chance this monopolistic power comes to grief the world could (I do not venture to predict that it would) be so over-supplied with diamonds as to bring down prices probably to less than fifty per cent. of those which now rule.   This is not a mere opinion, but those who know better than I profess

Q

to do the amount of possible production consider it a certainty. Kimberley is still a prosperous little place, no longer, indeed, progressing by leaps and bounds, but very well to do.

Little or no demand for additional white labour exists, then, at present, neither is the locality attractive to the eye, although it is only just to say that it would be difficult to discover anywhere in South Africa a heartier or more genial set of people than the inhabitants of the diamond-producing centre.

A curiously marked characteristic of the South African situation is that when ruin seems inevitable something which may be called, for the want of a better term, a fluke occurs, and the crash is averted. The discovery of diamonds saved the Cape Colony; and just as the Transvaal had reached the lowest grade of poverty and degradation, some ten years or so ago, the discovery of the wonderful deposits of gold in and around the Witwater's Randt district saved the country from the utter smash which seemed so nearly impending, and Johannesburg has become—in spite of every possible obstacle the Transvaal autocrat, Kruger, and his myrmidons could oppose—a handsome and prosperous city, which bids fair to take high rank some day in the civilised world. That day will not be during the Krugerian reign, if any human antagonism counts.

This brutally ignorant tyrant is the very worst danger to his state—it is more than absurd to call it a republic—possible. His own dear burghers are too ignorant to discover the patent fact that he is, as far as they are concerned, simply acting the wolf costumed as a sheep, and that he is quite cunning enough to carry on his ruthless game likely to be undetected by them for an indefinite period, so they must pay the penalty as best may be. As for the European and advanced Africander population, those of their numbers who are un-subsidised in some way know full well that their noses will be put to the grindstone by Oom Paul when opportunity serves, and for the present make the best use they can of things in general. Every intending immigrant to the Transvaal should be made aware of the fact that at present he would represent a superfluity, as hundreds of capable aspirants for work, skilled and unskilled, are incapable of finding it, and, although the wages of those already employed look tempting in print, they represent a very insufficient purchasing power in a place where almost everything is three times dearer than in England.

Comfort, except in the case of rich people, is an unknown quantity in or near the gold fields, and upon the whole, or for the present at least, I should feel guilty of cruelty if I held out any encouragement for immigration thither in the general sense of the word, although perhaps an exceptionally lucky skilled artisan may do well.

Had Mr. Gladstone after Majuba subordinated his sentimental proclivities to the maintenance of the interest, the honour, and the prestige of his country, and refrained from giving back the Transvaal to the Boers, he could easily have done so without bloodshed, and in all probability tens of thousands of Englishmen in excess of the present population would have made South Africa their home; but instead of that he preferred perpetrating one of the very few jokes he has been guilty of, and labelled it "Magnanimity." The joke fell flat: it was too grim for any but Boers to appreciate, but they at least laughed as heartily as their gloomy temperaments permitted. It may be taken for granted that South African prosperity depends wholly and solely on her mineral resources, as her other assets are too insignificant, and too unsusceptible of any really material augmentation, to count for much relatively to her indebtedness. Fortunately there seems to be no reason to fear that the output of gold will show any decrease for many years to come, and every reason to feel confident that a great increase in that output will be annually realised for an indefinite but certainly long period.

The future of the diamond fields, although hopeful, is less certain of a lengthy state of prosperous endurance, simply because the. supply of these stones largely exceeds demands, and the profits on them at present rates are only maintained by artificial means—some of which are iniquitous, and all in conflict with the tradition and customs of modern commerce. Moreover, these gems do not wear out, and at best are merely ornamental adjuncts of the toilettes of the more foolish or of the more vulgar classes, bear no interest, and lock up a very considerable amount of capital, which would otherwise be more beneficially employed.

Intending settlers in any part of South Africa

may possibly bear the foregoing remarks in mind, as the prosperity of individuals here hinges entirely on that of these mining centres and the commerce they engender.

British capital is already invested to an enormous amount in these mining industries and in the commerce they have initiated, but there is plenty of room for an indefinite amount of increased investments if only means could be found to induce, or compel, the Transvaal autocracy to modify its intense animosity to Britons and their interests, originating, or at any rate intensified, by the fact that Paul Kruger and his burghers are indebted to English generosity for their present position and for every shilling they own, and are, for no other reason than the fact that they are under the greatest obligation to her, determined to verify the old adage that an obligee is usually not only ungrateful but hostile to the benefactor.

The present Transvaal situation is about as follows:—

A flourishing mining centre has been established by Britons and other Europeans (Uitlanders), and, if unchecked in its prosperous course, a largely increased population of these detested Gibeonites is certain, and will not only threaten the continuance in power of the notoriously corrupt Boer officialdom but the existence of the state itself. The policy of its rulers therefore is, if possible, to limit progress within its present bounds, by rendering it impossible to work at any profit any but the very best mines, which are already numerous enough to afford a sufficiently manageable looting area for Paul and his Bashi-Bazouks, out of which he and his constituency have realised many ill-gotten millions. As a field for immigration at present South Africa may be considered congested so long as the Transvaal Executive is allowed to persist in obstructing the influx of capital with a view to maintain present conditions as near as possible intact, and the revenues derivable from the working of the best class of mines only being quite sufficient to satisfy even the personal miserly characteristics of the President, to provide handsome fortunes for the higher officials, and to square such members of the Raad as may be necessary to secure a majority when requisite.

To allow the less profitable grade of reefs to be developed—which they most certainly would be with improved political and legislative circumstances—would simply mean the influx of the hated Uitlanders in sufficient numbers to imperil the existence of the miserable force which under the name of government is allowed to paralyse South African industries and commerce, and which will some day bring about a tragedy should any little pretext be found—say, for instance, a noisy political meeting or a street riot—for ordering a rifle fire to be poured on the helpless Johannesburg crowd.

The desire for such an opportunity has more than once been expressed by the members of the Raad; in it are men who would be delighted to earn promotion by any barbarity of the kind, and the perpetration of which would be a sure method of obtaining it. That such a Liliputian with such a mere handful of ignorant Boers should be allowed to dominate the destinies of South Africa is not merely ludicrous but palpably dangerous, not only in the way above mentioned, but even more so as being another perilous trial of the loyalty of the British and advanced Africanders, who have so often been made the scapegoats of temporary Imperial exigencies. To limit the discussion of Transvaal questions within a radius of quibbles about suzerainty, conventions, and paramountcy is absurd, and a mere waste of time. Mental ophthalmia is prevalent enough in South Africa, but, after all, the complaint is not so eternally endemic as to obscure the vision of intelligent Colonists, who are rapidly losing faith in palliatives, and demand a cure. Let it not be supposed that I advocate a warlike solution of the Transvaal question, which indeed might be necessary but certainly regrettable.

Paul Kruger is puffed up with the ideas of assistance from Germany, but although the Kaiser is a very amusing and accomplished young gentleman, he would not count for much as a meddler in South African affairs, even could he be unwise enough to run the risk of active interference. It is safe to assert—and prove—that ever since the Transvaal retrocession the attitude of its rulers has been one of undiluted hostility to England, augmenting day by day in proportion to the impunity extended, till it has now reached a point which, as regards the interests of commerce, is fast becoming unendurable. In addition to this, on every possible occasion insults such as no other country than England would for a moment have

hesitated to demand and obtain satisfaction for
have been submitted to by the so-called "paramount" South African Power. A member of the
President's family, in the service of the Executive,
has been ostentatiously promoted simply because
he vituperated our Gracious Queen, not only as a
sovereign but as a woman, in language which would
have shocked even the most erudite in Billingsgate
slang. Other officials of less note have been
equally fortunate in that they supplied our enemies
in war-time with ammunition and other assistance.
And so things jolt along somehow for the present,
but the time must soon come when everybody
interested in the prosperity of South Africa or in
the honour or prestige of the Empire will demand
that the Transvaal Government shall be wheeled
into line, compelled to become a humble unit in
the ranks of civilised nations, or be incorporated
once for all within Imperial limits. I sincerely
hope that no one will come to the conclusion that
I am prejudiced against the Boers, as a community.
Indeed, I ought to know them well, and I feel
convinced that under improved political and social
circumstances they are capable of unlimited improvement, as their faults, such as they are, are

mostly the outcome of traditional education and by the influence of a narrow-minded, essentially bigoted, and self-seeking hierarchy acute enough to take every advantage of the superstitious elements so naturally resulting from ignorance and isolation in the grim solitudes of African surroundings and scenery, and to exploit them for its own peculiar benefit. The Boers have been accused en masse of invincible laziness and want of enterprise by those of our countrymen who have gathered ideas of them during flying visits, and failed to estimate the distinction between causes and effects. It is true enough that the Boer is devoid of that bustling and restless activity so remarkable in the Briton; it is also true that when his experience of the nature of things he has to deal with permits him to hope for reward he is as industrious as anybody else, and so thrifty by nature, or habit, as to make the most of the very moderate success which an adverse nature allows on the Dark Continent. The year 1897 has been one of frightful suffering to the poor Boers, thousands of whom have lost their all from rinderpest, locusts, and drought.

Hundreds of these poor people have died of sheer

starvation ; thousands have succumbed to fever and other diseases incident to an insufficient diet largely composed of wild roots. The quality of brave and silent suffering is wonderfully developed in the Boer race; as an eyewitness I might cite many harrowing proofs in evidence. If only a modicum of the distress and misery among the Boers inhabiting the northern and western districts of the Transvaal had occurred in any British dependency, effective steps would have been taken to meet the situation. Imbued with the convenient creed that Providence has decreed these misfortunes, and that it would savour of sin seriously to assist the sufferers, the Transvaal Government has only ventured on applying the most homœopathic palliatives, with, of course, little or no beneficial result.

The wealth-gorged President groaningly contributed £5 to help his dear burghers; at last a small show was made to avoid the scandal of appearing utterly indifferent.

A mass of the surviving Boer sufferers has surged into the mining centres in search of employment, but as the Government doggedly clings to its policy of limiting the industry there, these poor people have merely exchanged the frying-pan for the fire ; if press accounts are credible, the existing misery and mortality among them is awful, and is much more likely to continue than to abate.

I will therefore venture to reiterate my advice to intending emigrants to South Africa by a repetition of the word " Don't."

CHAPTER XIII.

BOER MARKSMANSHIP.

THE idea that every Boer is a first-class rifle shot seems to have become a form of faith, in its way, in England, and I am afraid that no observations of mine will have much effect in dispelling the prevalent credulity on this subject.

It is, however, perfectly true that when the Transvaal was a game country the majority of these people acquired a certain amount of aptitude, as distinct from exact skill, in the use of their weapons, and that the natural deficiencies of their country, from every agricultural and pastoral point of view, made it more or less necessary, in order to fill the pot and neutralise the vituperative instincts of the " Vrouw," that the males of the family should stand to their arms ; thus many of them attained a certain amount of skill in the use of guns, although very few could claim to be really good shots.

Upon the whole, however, it may fairly be conceded that a formidable amount of aggregate skill in the use of their weapons was a noticeable characteristic of the Boers of the period I allude to (say twenty years ago), and at the time of the Boer war with us all the middle-aged men, and a good many of the youngsters, were as a rule, and as compared with trained soldiers, very efficient shots and formidable as guerillas, not only on account of their marksmanship, but from the possession of that skill in choosing positions, and taking advantage of every chance offered, which is acquired by all hunters sooner or later, but is hardly susceptible of being taught on systematic lines to large bodies of men.

While the game lasted in the Transvaal, every hale man was more or less a hunter, and the majority of the burghers lapsed into poverty, very nearly approaching absolute pauperism, when about seventeen or eighteen years ago the game herds were no longer numerous enough to be profitably exploited.

Gradually but swiftly extinction has supervened, and the Transvaal is no longer a happy hunting ground for any but Jews. With the virtual extermination of the larger kinds of game in the Transvaal, the Boers in a great measure ceased the pursuit of the scattered remnants of the survivors, and soon became but little interested in keeping up their efficiency as riflemen.

As a matter of fact, since the general introduction of long-range, breechloading weapons, their shooting powers have steadily deteriorated, and from having been as a rule fairly good rough performers, the younger members of this generation have ceased to take any interest in field sports, and as regards rifle shooting are mere duffers. Indeed, ever since the modern rifle came into general use in the Transvaal, the Boers have gradually lost that amount of skill as shootists upon which their prestige was founded in former days.

The extreme ease with which breechloading rifles can be loaded, and the long range of these weapons, contributed largely to the deterioration of their original skill by inducing habits of carelessness as to distances, and a preference for pumping a stream of lead into the "brown" without much regard to aim. This soon makes the game animals very wild, and, in proportion to the number of cartridges expended, very little game is gathered, and an enormous waste by wounding occurs, as few hunters care to follow game animals wounded at distances which mean, at any rate, a long and uncertain stern chase, and mostly end in failure.

Even in their palmiest days as hunters very few Boers could be reckoned as first-class shots, although most of them could account for a good deal of game, the result not so much of their shooting skill as their aptitude in negotiating difficult and somewhat dangerous ground on their active and well-trained shooting horses.

At times I have hunted a good deal with the Boers, but of first-class performers among them can only remember some half-dozen who came nearly up to that mark, and strangely enough none of that number used modern weapons. Indeed, two of them stuck to flint and steel till their deaths some few years ago.

In support of my poor opinion of Boer shooting, I may mention that shortly after the introduction of breechloading rifles with brass cartridge-cases

I spent a month or so with some Boers who were hunting on the banks of the Limpopo. Their party consisted of three brothers, who with their wives and children had camped for the winter, to hunt chiefly for hides, and for the benefit of their cattle, as the pasture was good, and game sufficiently plentiful. They were a good, kindly lot, and considered first-rate shots. Being men of only average weight, and well mounted, they did a lot of hunting every forenoon except on Sunday. Their arms consisted of breechloading ·450 rifles.

Observing the vast number of cartridges they expended, as compared with the tale of game brought in, I took the opportunity of ascertaining approximately the number of shots fired during one week, and the result was that each head of game gathered had cost about thirty cartridges, and I think this fairly represents the average performances of Boer hunters.

On a previous occasion, when in want of buffalo hides, I hired a young Boer with a good reputation as a game shot to help me, and although he killed some game to feed our Kaffirs before we found buffaloes, I noticed that he wasted a good deal of ammunition. As I had to feed his 12-bore gun,

I counted the bullets supplied daily when we at last got among the buffaloes and shot at no other game. Upon these animals my companion expended fifty-six bullets, of which about fifty were wasted.

As we shot on foot (on account of the presence of the tsetse-fly), this was very poor work, taking into consideration the abundance of the game, their unusual tameness, and that the locality was admirably adapted to stalking requirements.

On this occasion, instead of being in one huge mass, the buffaloes were scattered about in more or less small groups all over the country, near the numerous rain pools, and were almost as easy to kill as if they had been domestic cattle. Probably this lot had never before been under fire, as they merely shifted about, instead of quitting the ground en masse as big game usually does when it has smelt powder.

As I have an aversion to shooting in company, I did not witness my friend's operations, but his Kaffir attendants said that his want of success was occasioned by his predilection for long shots; and to make a good bag of big game, close quarters and very straight powder are a sine qua non.

The extraordinary vitality of all kinds of African game animals counts, however, for much as regards the usual discrepancy between the amount of ammunition expended and its practical effects.

Details on such subjects are, however, rather too ghastly to be put into type, and would moreover approach the incredible too nearly to venture on in print with any hope of escaping imputations of an undesirable nature.

For my own part, on this occasion I used a heavy smooth-bore double gun, and did not fire a shot at more than about forty yards, and never pulled off till the sights focussed on a fatal spot, as a wounded buffalo is the most dangerous animal in the world, bar none—in my opinion.

The reader must not, however, conclude that the Boers are nearly such vile shots as the figures I have quoted would indicate, bearing in mind the fact that all African game animals, with the exception of the pachyderms and buffalo, are very much wilder, swifter, and more on the alert than those in any other parts of the world I have seen or read of, and that a steady shot at a motionless animal is of very rare occurrence.

The extraordinary tenacity of life in all African

game, with the exception of the obese eland, also counts for much in extenuation of the small bags as compared with the ammunition expended in obtaining them, and all I wish to make clear is that the Boers are by no means the marvellous riflemen they are supposed to be, although in their way good enough to compare favourably in shooting powers with the brave but inept British Tommy Atkins, and that every day they are " going off " their shooting, for the reasons given above, inclusive of the fact that the cost of modern rifle ammunition militates against sufficient practice with their weapons for the mere purpose of keeping up to the mark as rifle experts.

The extermination of game in and near the Transvaal has also reduced the majority of the poorer and more efficient burghers to the position of unskilled labourers too hard pressed to keep the wolf from the door to afford leisure for the practice of rifle shooting, and they may now be fairly considered as " out of it " as regards anything approaching exceptional skill as marksmen.

My opinion in these respects is, I think, cor-roborated by the results of their fire in the late combat with Dr. Jameson's raiders. On this occasion the Boers fired from behind rocks, which protected them completely from the effects of the horizontal fire of the enemy, whom they could pot at on an exposed plain on which marks indicating distances had been placed. Moreover, the poor raiders and their horses were too exhausted by hunger, thirst, and long marches to be able to attempt either an assautl or a retreat; and yet, with all this in their favour, these redoubtable burghers were only able to kill twenty-two of Dr. Jameson's men, in addition to a few minor casualties, with an expenditure of, at the very least, 6,000 cartridges. The result can, therefore, only rank as a record of very poor shooting at best.

Had these burghers shot up to anything like their reputation for skill, they would have swept the plain of all but the killed and wounded in a few minutes—with, perhaps, a very few exceptions.

Reverting to some of the incidents which occurred during the buffalo hunt in the fly country, I can confidently say that although since then more years have elapsed than I care to count, my recollection of the experience is as vivid as if the occurrence had been quite a recent event, as many of the eventualities were exceptional and unique among my experiences.

For instance, just before reaching the edge of the "fly" district, some of the wild Kaffirs known to hunters as "Vaalpense" reported the arrival in the infested country of an unusually numerous herd of buffalo, which they thought had migrated from distant lands unknown to hunters with firearms, as they appeared very tame, and had located themselves in sparse bush, which is quite exceptional with the habits of these animals when they have once smelt powder.

Naturally the marvellous accounts these people gave us of the incredible numbers of the herds were received with numerous "grains of salt," but having completed camping arrangements, and arranged for the portage of the necessary impedimenta, we were soon tramping for the indicated locality, accompanied by a large gang of Kaffirs, with their wives and such of their children as were big enough to stand the fatigue of a long day's waterless march with impunity; and having started at dawn, we duly arrived at the indicated locality soon after dark, and were glad, after coffee and a scanty meal, to curl up in the best shelter available, without troubling to make the usual shelters (skerms), and soon were in the land of Nod amid the blazing fires of the bivouac.

Next morning, numerous fresh "spoors" of buffalo were visible near our night quarters, and soon we viewed such numbers of the game we were in quest of, scattered in groups all over the country within the range of vision, that the Kaffirs' reports were amply verified.

Leaving my companion to choose his own course, I went on in the opposite direction, and before noon had killed nine buffaloes, and returned alone to the bivouac to recruit, leaving Kaffirs at each carcase to skin and cut the meat into portable shape.

I met with no adventures of a dangerous nature during this hunt, probably because of the absence of any thick cover. In a jungly country buffaloes are the most dangerous of all African game, as in such situations wounded animals have a habit of concealing themselves and of pouncing out upon any one they catch a glimpse of with extraordinary rapidity, and unless a suitable tree is at hand to climb into, the man is nearly certain to come to grief even if well armed, as a front shot at a charging buffalo, owing to the peculiar position the head is then held in, is rarely effective, although it sometimes turns the enraged brute out of his direct course, and saves the man who is near a climbable tree, which is then sometimes blockaded by the buffalo, perhaps for hours, in the event of the loss of his weapons by the intended victim during the scrimmage or the climb. As I have been " treed " more than once, I can assure the reader that the entire evolution is sufficiently unpleasant until one is at least several feet above the pursuer's reach.

In a fairly open country buffaloes rarely charge home, and on the hunt I am now treating of no accident happened, but after we returned to the waggons, and were busy drying the hides, a couple of Kaffirs offered to barter a hide, and we came to terms. The couple then left the camp to bring in the spoil, and late on the following day only one returned, looking abject enough.

The story was that he and his chum thought they had seen a badly wounded buffalo during our march back to the camp, and that they should find him dead and strip him of his armour. In fact, they found him lying apparently defunct, and one of them, to make sure, threw an assegai at him, on the receipt of which the dying animal suddenly sprang up, pinned the poor Kaffir, and shortly pounded him into pulp. During this horrible process the survivor had " treed " close by, and when the wounded beast had again lain down, decamped from his perch and made hasty tracks for the camp, leaving the dead to be buried by the vultures and other carnivora.

Subsequently we heard that the bony remains of this buffalo and his victim had been found, and so ended the tragedy.

In the days I have alluded to, troops of buffaloes of from fifty to two hundred or so were common enough, but the numbers met with on this trip far exceeded anything of the kind within any of my experiences in the hunting fields, and, moreover, several more or less numerous troops of giraffe were dotted over the parklike country, not to mention abundance of minor game, such as brindled gnus, hartebeest, sassabi, a few ostriches, and a lot of the pallah antelope, multiplied the attractions of the show.

As usual in " fly " districts, lions did not turn up, and only a few stale spoors of them were seen. This may be accounted for, probably, by the fact that lions spend their nights in hunting and gorging and their days in slumber, the enjoyment of which is materially diminished no doubt by the incessant and painful attacks of the tsetse.

A few days sufficed to dry and pack our hides and other spolia, the amount of which severely taxed the transport department, even after leaving the Kaffirs happy in the possession of several tons of their favourite "naama" (meat), with which the trees and bushes around were festooned in strips, in process of becoming "belting" in the dry and fervid atmosphere. Not a scrap of meat was wasted, and we left our sable friends secure of enjoying their ideas of Utopia for several weeks at least.

Having of late noticed in the sporting press that various attempts are being made to establish sanctuaries for the protection of African game animals, in which a restricted amount of shooting will be conditionally permitted, I may say that I cordially approve of the proposed action to be taken by those interested. Perhaps I may escape a verdict for presumption if I venture to suggest that the effective protection of African game is hardly possible if permits are granted to mounted hunters, and that therefore no horses should on any pretext be allowed to be taken within the prescribed limits of game sanctuaries, as it is a patent fact that horsemen cause a very appreciable amount of destruction by random firing, and wounding, without gathering, vast numbers of the game, and perhaps even more by driving the herds out of the limits of accessibility.

In fact, it is safe to say that whereas foot hunters merely decimate game, mounted parties exterminate it permanently and rapidly. Moreover, it should be made obligatory on all persons receiving permits to hunt in protected localities to remove all elevating back sights from their weapons other than a fixed standard one for one hundred yards, and that the sights so removed be deposited for safe keeping with a duly accredited official, responsible for their return to the owners at a period to be arranged for.

Furthermore, it would be most desirable to get a law made by the dominant power in the localities adverted to, making it a penal offence for any unlicensed person, irrespective of colour, to be found in possession of firearms (revolvers and pistols for defensive purposes excepted) within limits to be made known by proclamation.

Even where expense is only a secondary consideration, I think wire fencing would fail to confine game within definite limits, as pachyderms and buffaloes would go through it with little more inconvenience than they would feel in passing through cobwebs — barbs notwithstanding — and through outlets made by them lighter game would levant too.

Before closing this chapter, it may interest some readers to be informed that the inherent pioneering instinct of our Dutch fellow colonists is again finding vent in a " trek " of considerable dimensions to N'Gaamiland, which is probably now (May, 1898) struggling through the Great South African Thirst Land towards its goal in the north-west.

This "trek" was initiated by a Dutch padre named Hoffmeyer, and it is said he is to join it in the capacity of the pastor of the adventurers. If this is true, he will achieve a record, as' his reverend brethren in South Africa have hitherto been mainly distinguished for a limpet-like adherence to localities, where this position secures them a degree of comfort, and even luxury uncommon enough hereaway, outside the million-aire ranks, and abundant leisure, the normal con-dition 'of their professional existence ; and it is safe to say that in N'Gaamiland a totally different state of things will prevail at least for a very long time.

Be this as it may, let us hope the " trekkers " will have better luck than those who preceded them some years ago, and of whose sufferings from sickness, hunger, and thirst I was an eyewitness during the retreat of the survivors from their hoped-for Canaan.

Personally, I think the immense district I am alluding to is unfit for settlement for whites, as the more fertile parts, such as the Botletle Valley and near the lake, are eminently malarial, a very fatal form of fever prevailing during the greater part of the year, and the healthier parts are but scantily watered by little springs, with immense intervals between them as a rule.

From an African point of view, the pastoral capabilities of the country now in question are decidedly better than the usual average in South Africa, and all species of stock flourish, with the exception of horses and mules, which die like flies during and after the rains, and if the Boer immigrants want to ride they will have to content themselves on the backs of trained oxen, or, in the case of light-weights, on the dorsal ridge of asinine mounts.

A more uninviting country to the eye would indeed be difficult to find outside the Arctic regions, but the Boer is utterly insensible either of the charms of the picturesque or of their absence. Good pasture and a sufficiency of indifferent water suffice to make him a happy smoker of the calumet of content.

Gold, or diamonds, or both, may possibly be discovered, but the possibility of converting them into profitable assets is hardly obvious.

CHAPTER XIV.

POSTSCRIPT: THE POLITICAL SITUATION.

SINCE the foregoing chapters have been in the printer's hands Paul Kruger has been re-elected nominally as President of the Transvaal, but really as its Autocrat; no doubt the majority of that large section of the British public interested in South African affairs will consider the fact as a more or less genuine expression of the public opinion of the Burgher constituency as especially accentuated by the immense majority of votes polled for this rustic potentate. The sooner, however, that opinion is discarded by Officialdom, and by those interested in the expansion of British commerce, in the reinstatement of the indispensable "prestige" so recklessly thrown to the winds by Mr. Gladstone's Administration, and in the peace and welfare of the country generally, the better for all concerned.

The re-election itself was a foregone conclusion, and merely the natural result of the utter absence of public opinion on political and social exigencies among the ignorant and superstitious majority of the miserable little electorate. Those who know the inner workings of the Boer mind (such as it is) are well aware of the fact that although Paul Kruger is by no means so popular among them as he is generally supposed to be by outsiders, they have been drilled to attach to his name a sort of loyalty as representing a personage specially appointed by Providence as one to be obeyed, and that disobedience to this mandate would simply mean sin and its punishment. The small section of the electorate who are more or less sceptical on this point is, of course, easily dealt with by such a man as Dr. Leyds at the helm of the state's ship, and the humble helot Uitlander, in the absence of efficient recognition by representatives of his national government, as easily made to pay the piper.

It has been said that nothing short of a surgical operation is effective to enable a Scot to appreciate a joke, and it is clear to my mind at least that, whatever may be the truth as regards the gallant Scot, the Boer as represented by Paul Kruger will never be capable of understanding his own interests as they are affected by political action. Much less will he care to expend a thought on those of others, in the absence of the fear of surgical appliances to the traditional endemic disease of his mental constitution.

The present condition of things in the Transvaal under the existing régime is bad enough, and will sooner or later become intolerable unless radically reformed from the outside. It would seem advisable, in the interests of South Africa and of Imperial Britain, that no more time should be wasted in hairsplitting and futile controversy on questions as to the meaning of the word "suzerainty," or as to that of this or that clause in the miserable Conventions of which we know, and ought to be ashamed.

It has always been apparent that one of the chief impediments to adequate action in South African affairs on the part of the Imperial Government has been an exaggerated fear of the consequences of meddling with an assumed racial antipathy between the English and Africander population of the Cape Colony and of South Africa generally. I by no means endorse this idea, and have every reason to believe that the two races would get on extremely well together were it not for the action of certain political agitators and minor cliques interested in the maintenance of a profitable fiction. It must, however, be admitted that in South Africa the Imperial Government in bygone days committed about as many blunders as the nature of the situation admitted, and that this has complicated the existing knot to such an extent that attempts to untie it can only end in its severance once for all, and the adoption of less tortuous and more honest action in the future.

The present situation of South Africa as affected by the inimical action of the Transvaal potentate is briefly this. An immense auriferous area exists which if developed would in a very short time double the present value of all the commercial interests of the country and make a very considerable advantageous increase in English commerce generally, and increasingly as the years pass by. At present, large as the export of gold is, only a few first-class mines pay dividends, but the majority of inferior grades would soon do so were it not that the Transvaal policy is to take effectual measures to overburden the industry with excessive taxation in various forms. The natural influx of capital is thus effectually dammed, immigration stopped, and trade seriously depressed.

There is no excuse for this condition of things, which, while it obstructs general progress of the Uitlanders, will also soon pauperise the Boers. The continued vitality of the Krugerian régime is fostered by the non-interventionary attitude of the Imperial Government, which, however, can hardly be condoned in view of the manifest dangers which augmentingly threaten the peace and prosperity of the entire South African dependencies.

That such a state of things should be allowed to exist in this century, simply that one notorious miser, who has never known the meaning of one generous impulse, may pile up his useless hoards, and that a few of his satellites may accumulate large fortunes by pillaging the helot Uitlanders, is, to say the least of it, disgraceful, especially when we know that the necessary administrative expenses of government in the Transvaal, under proper control, need not cost much more than one-third of the revenue now exacted. At least two-thirds of the Transvaal revenues represent merely funds for corrupt practices, or loans and casual assets are applied to pay for armaments as useless as they are minatory. I may say that the South African public has confidence in the existing Imperial Ministry, and add, with equal sincerity, that it is pretty certain that any recurrence to the tortuous sentimental impolicies of former days would be illustrated by the sorry spectacle of " wigs on the green."

Although cornered by the result of the unfortunate Jameson raid (which would, perhaps, have been dubbed a " coup d'état" if it had been successful), and as a consequence of the advantage of position accruing to Paul Kruger from the catastrophe, the vulpine cunning of the old Boer was more than a match for the diplomatic forms by which Mr. Chamberlain was bound in the subsequent discussion of the matter. Every one here who is worth recognition places the utmost confidence in his (Mr. Chamberlain's) honesty, ability, and patriotism.

Certain Ministerial utterances on the subject of the ridiculous and insulting terms of the indemnity demanded of the Chartered Company by the Transvaal Government encourage the hope that this subject will be treated on its merits without reference to any propitiatory sacrifice to Transvaal proclivities. That the details of the bill of costs handed in by Dr. Leyds could not be sworn to as correct without the commission of perjury by its concocters I feel sure, as I have some remembrance of the very small expense of calling out "commandos" in that part of the world, and am convinced that all costs of that kind have been covered by the fines inflicted on the officers implicated and by the value of the captured loot, and that a very nice little balance has been left over for the benefit of others. The charge of £28,000 for the benefit of the families of the five or six casualties to burghers in the fight with Dr. Jim is exorbitant, unless the Transvaal Government is prepared to stultify itself by proving that its official report of these casualties was false, and that the real losses of the Boers by death and wounds in the skirmish were infinitely greater than those on account of which the claim is based. For my own part I believe in the approximate correctness of the report, and that the loss of life among the burghers did not exceed five men, as not only are the Boers expert tacticians, but they are most unlikely to accept battle in any situation where they would not be comparatively exempt from danger.

As for the million demanded as compensation for the outraged moralities of the Transvaal, it would be beneath the dignity of either the Imperial Government or of the Chartered Company to discuss the item, but it will be difficult for those who will be called upon to adjudicate on the subject in question to restrain a hearty laugh when this item is reached. Statesmen, and men of business, are not generally supposed to be experts in the observation or delineation of such microscopic nebulosities as Dr. Leyds, Kruger, and Co. have so insolently presumed to introduce. Indeed, upon the whole, the Chartered Company might do worse than refuse to pay any fraction of the indemnity, but offer to close the matter by a handsome donation to the families of the dead and wounded Boers who suffered in the fight. Further, it would be a graceful act to vote a liberal sum for the relief of the semi-starvation of the multitudes of the Transvaal burghers who have suffered from the effects of rinderpest, locusts, drought, have been decimated by disease, hopelessly pauperised, and to whom but scant charity has been shown by their own Government. Some such course would probably commend itself to the British people.

Impartial readers of any true history of South Africa (assuming an entity which I doubt) will not fail to conclude that of all people the Boers, and more especially the Transvaal section of them, have every reason to be grateful to England, not only as having preserved their then helpless community from obliteration by Zulu assegais in Chetewayo's time, but as having conquered for them a valuable extent of country known as Seecoceonie's Country, where they had suffered severe defeat. It might also be well to remind the public at this juncture that although a large number of Boers took up raiding on British territory as an occupation, and during two years ravaged Stellaland and murdered British subjects, whites and blacks, in great numbers, only relinquishing the practice when the expedition under the command of Colonel Warren was sent against them, at an expense to England of more than a million of money, perfect immunity from punishment was granted to them, and no indemnity was even asked for. In view of these facts, it is difficult to estimate the amount of cheek which prompted the delivery of such an abnormal demand for indemnity on the part of the Transvaal, which, even if we exclude the morality item, amounts to no less than a fraud. The Jameson raid was over in a few days; no cattle or other property was looted; every Boer met with was treated well; and the raid itself was only an episode of the revolutionary attempts at Johannesburg, made with a view to mitigate intolerable conditions imposed by a Government living on a legalised system of plunder, and applying the greater part of the funds so acquired to enrich its personnel.

Even Paul Kruger, destitute as he is of any of the refined or generous instincts of an ordinary civilised Christian, might, cne would think, reflect advantageously on the fact that at least ninety-nine per cent. of the herd of golden calves he is now enabled to·worship are the produce of the sweat and industry and capital of the hated Uitlander, without which the treasures of the land would have been still embedded in its rocks, and he himself could have achieved no better position than that of the Presidency of a bankrupt state on a salary of, say, £800 a year at the utmost, the half of

which would have been paid in mealies (maize)
and other farm produce, collected with difficulty,
and paid in reluctantly, as in the cases of former
Presidents. No; if any case of the repudiation
of a claim was ever justifiable, the Chartered
Company and the Imperial Government would
only be exercising a right by refusing to discuss
the indemnity question in its present shape, if at
all, except perhaps in the form of a petition as
distinguished from a demand.

It might also be as well while existing differences
prevail to definitely express the precise meaning
of the word suzerainty by Act of Parliament, seeing
that the attitude of the Government of the Transvaal has now become a source of serious danger
to her Majesty's dominions in South Africa, and
has already compelled the augmentation of the
naval and military forces in this part of the world,
the extra charges for which ought to be debited
to the Transvaal failing a complete change for the
better in the attitude of its Autocrat and his clique.
To dilate in detail on the prevalent system cf
misrule in that country is beyond my present
purpose, but I hope I have said enough to be some
guide to the British public in forming its opinion

of the causes, and probably dangerous consequences, of the existing muddle in South African affairs which originated in the lamentable and disgraceful course of action of the Imperial Administration in power when white - feather politics were paramount. No Englishman wishes to interfere with Transvaal liberties or independence, but the authorities there ought to be candidly told that political liberty and licentiousness are two very distinct things, and that a persistence in the latter line of action will no longer be permitted as hitherto. This is the only sort of language which can be made comprehensible to the ordinary Boer brain, and it is devoutly to be hoped that he will not compel the meaning of it to be hammered into him, but will do justice to the Uitlander, repudiate his Chinese policy and habits of thought, bury the hatchet once for all, and put his sturdy shoulder to the wheel of progress instead of attempting to hinder its revolution as he has hitherto been taught to do.

For the second time during the last two years Paul Kruger is engaged in a serious quarrel with the Judicial Bench of the Transvaal, with the object of subjecting the decisions of the Courts to revision or annulment at the hands of the Executive—whenever it may appear desirable to the wirepullers, who are quite up to the ways and means of securing a majority in the Raad sufficient to pass any law dictated by its despot. This has always been the aim of Oom Paul Kruger, who about ten years ago exercised this species of dispensing power without even the pretence of having it legalised, in the case of one Nelmapius, a Hollander, and protégé of his, who had been sentenced by the High Court to imprisonment for embezzlement of public funds. In this case the President personally went to the gaol and released the prisoner without vouchsafing any explanation. The then Chief Justice resigned as a matter of course, and although a little flutter of excitement occurred, and a few adverse comments on the subject appeared in the local Press, Kruger triumphed, and Nelmapius shortly afterwards died a free man in the country whose criminal laws he had been found guilty of outraging. In the case now pending the Chief Justice Kotze has been dismissed summarily for attempting opposition to the Krugerian will. Mr. Kotze, who is respected for his acknowledged legal abilities and for his upright character, is now fighting for the general principle involved by the attempt of the Executive to legalise the dispensing power, and deserves the unstinted support of the public ; as, if this attempt on the part of Kruger is successful, all security for life and property in the Transvaal vanishes, and the President and his clique supersede the law to all intents and purposes.

Comment on such a possible state of things is superfluous. It will be a question for jurists to decide whether such an infraction of the law is or is not an infraction of existing Conventions ; but there can be no doubt that should the Transvaal Executive become paramount, the interests of the whole of the people of South Africa, and those of investors in South African properties, will be seriously endangered. In such circumstances it seems clear that the question changes its character as a local grievance and becomes of national importance, and, as such, one to be dealt with by the Imperial Government.

The population of Johannesburg and of other mining centres here has been so helotised of late that any energetic local action is hardly to be expected in the absence of effectual outside

support, but surely petitions to the Imperial
Government embodying a statement of all
existing grievances and requesting its assistance
in an endeavour to procure substantial reforms is
indicated, and should be attempted.   ·

Expert jurists may perhaps be able to discover
the difference between a state subject to the
suzerainty of a monarch and of a feudatory one
" pur et simple." Any plain man of fairly good
mental capacity will probably come to the conclusion that although some possible difference
may be discoverable, no adverse distinction is
obvious. Assuming this as a fact, it becomes clear
that the right to interfere in supreme cases is
unquestionable ; it is equally clear that the question
at issue between the British population of the
Transvaal and of the Government of the
Uitlanders generally, and of all investors in
property in South Africa, renders the case urgent.
Surely a monarch is within his or her right in
interfering with a view to avert a palpable danger
to the peace and prosperity of an Empire and its
dependencies when these are threatened by the
action of an unfriendly feudatory state.

It must be by no means inferred from the

foregoing expression of my opinion on the subject treated that I am advocating any interference with the conduct of the internal affairs of the Transvaal. Her Majesty's Ministers are not scavengers, and cannot be supposed to have any wish to bedaub themselves by any attempt to intermeddle with such an accumulation of Augean corruption as such action would entail. The actions and animus of the Transvaal Government are as hostile to British interests as a declaration of war would be, and no temperate but firm defensive remonstrances or measures taken by the Imperial Government to put an end to, or at least to mitigate the evils of the situation can by any means be construed into an interference with the internal government of the country. It must not be forgotten that approximately two-thirds of the Transvaal soil is owned by Englishmen and a few Europeans of other nationalities, whose sole dependence for protection . in very probable emergencies depends upon the action of the paramount power in South Africa. These people will soon be at the mercy of a vindictive despot and his subordinates, should Paul Kruger obtain the power of dispensing with the paramountcy of

Law and the substitution of Executive action in its place, although duly formulated by the farce of its endorsement by a Raad he has made wholly subservient to his orders—for a consideration. A few individuals of this body may be considered as in opposition to Krugerian policy, but they are only an impotent minority, with whom Oom Paul sometimes condescends to get into one of his ludicrous passions, but generally ignores, as he can well afford to do.

I have described the existent situation in the Transvaal as dangerous, and knowing as I do the characters of some of the prominent members of this precious Raad, and of the atrocious conduct they were prepared to exhibit at a certain memorable crisis in Transvaal history had the expressing the opinion that I am justified in expressing the opinion that I am justified in considering that allegation is well founded. The future of South Africa will be, I think, largely dependent on the action of the Chartered Company, if Rhodesia is proved to be the valuable country it is believed to be. Undoubtedly as a pastoral country it is infinitely superior to the Transvaal, and if the company could see its way to encourage Boer immigration, it would soon drain off the greater part of the best sort of the burghers of that nominal republic. Liberal monetary sacrifices as regards quit rents, and the like, would certainly be necessary on the part of the Company as a commencement, and a minimum employment of the red tape so hateful to the Boers would be prudent; but the ultimate success of some such well-devised scheme may, I think, be safely predicted.

In that case the company might justly consider itself as having been the factor of the much-to-be desired union of the white races in South Africa, which would be a consequence of the action hinted at; and this great objective of the founder of Rhodesia would be in a fair way to become another of his achievements, should he incline to use the great influence he possesses in favour of the plan of campaign here indicated.

THE END.

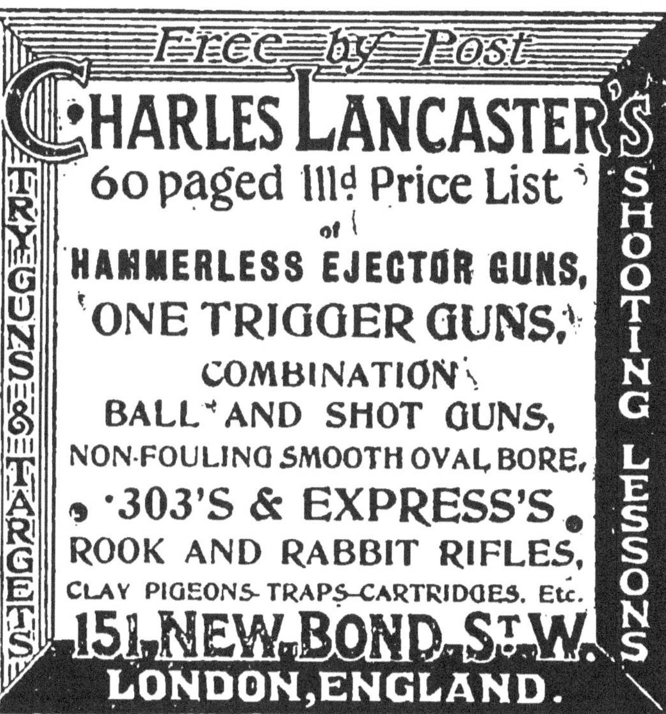

Free by Post
CHARLES LANCASTER'S
60 paged Illd Price List
of
HAMMERLESS EJECTOR GUNS,
ONE TRIGGER GUNS,
COMBINATION
BALL AND SHOT GUNS,
NON-FOULING SMOOTH OVAL BORE,
·303'S & EXPRESS'S
ROOK AND RABBIT RIFLES,
CLAY PIGEONS-TRAPS-CARTRIDGES. Etc.
151, NEW BOND St. W.
LONDON, ENGLAND.
TRY GUNS & TARGETS
SHOOTING LESSONS

ELEY'S

SPORTING

CARTRIDGES.

Eley's Waterproof Cartridge Case,

"PEGAMOID" PATENT.

ADVANTAGES:

Absolutely unaffected in wet weather.

Moisture cannot possibly get to the powder charge.

Cases do not swell even after being left on damp ground all night.

The turnover does not become loose.

To be had from ALL GUNMAKERS.   Wholesale only.

THE GUN AND ITS DEVELOPMENT,

By W. W. GREENER.

The Standard Work on Guns and Shooting.

Sixth Edition.

Revised and brought down to Date with many Additions, containing some 550 Illustrations, 750 Pages.

Price 10/6.

"THE GUN AND ITS DEVELOPMENT" contains a full history of Early Firearms, Cannon, and Gunpowder, and traces the evolution of the Modern Military Rifle and Sporting Shot Gun. No point of interest is left unnoticed, and the work has been thoroughly revised, added to, and brought down to date by varied additions. A voluminous Index enables the reader to refer instantly to any subject treated of in this Cyclopedia of Gunnery.

MODERN SHOT GUNS.

A Scientific Treatise on Guns and their Shooting,
By W. W. GREENER.

Second Edition. Cloth, Gilt Letters, Price 5s.

This treatise tells sportsmen just what they wish to know about guns; by reading it they will learn which guns to avoid, how to load their weapons to best advantage, how to keep them in repair, and how to benefit from their use.

Also to be obtained in German, Spanish and Italian Languages.

THE BREECHLOADER AND HOW TO USE IT.

WITH NOTES ON RIFLES.   By W. W. GREENER.

Seventh Edition just published. Price 3s. 6d. Cloth, 2s. 6d. Paper boards. Post Free.

390 Pages, copiously Illustrated (Cassell & Co.) (The First Edition of 5,000 sold in Four Months.)

The Book contains much information relative to the choice of guns, the detection of spurious and worthless weapons, and many practical hints on the handling and use of guns.

The text is illustrated with numerous woodcuts, many of them specially engraved for this work, the positions taken by renowned trap shots are shown, and the handling of the gun is pictorially illustrated; the aim of the author being to induce all who are interested in shooting to take an active part in this manly sport, and to advance the interests of all who look to the gun for pleasure, health or recreation.

May be obtained from all Booksellers, or the Author,

W. W. GREENER,

At 68, Haymarket, London, S.W., and St. Mary's Square, Birmingham.